The Sexual Exploits

of a Nympho

 PUBLICATIONS

www.rjpublications.net

ISBN: 0-9769277-2-1

For comments or to contact the author via email
rjeantay@yahoo.com

Acknowledgements

I would like to start by saying thanks to my parents for bringing me into this world. I would like to specifically thank my father for stepping up to the plate to play his role as a dad when I was a kid. Some men act like it's a choice, but it was never a choice with you.

I would like to thank all my friends who supported me and even those who haven't because it gives me great motivation to do even more with my life. The usual suspects who have been in my corner know who they are and I'm very grateful that you guys are still part of my life. I would like to send big hugs and kisses to my whole family, including my godson, nieces and nephews.

I can't forget Stacey Murphy. I'll continue to say that you're one in a million. I would like to thank my sister, Landgie, because her opinion is very valid to me. To my friends Carline, Elaine, Melissa, I hope that you guys can read the next one in a timely manner. I would also like to thank Francine for showing excitement about my work.

To the most important people associated with my writings, Marcus from Nubian Books, Massamba, Abo, Souleymon, Mory, Marlon and all the other book vendors and bookstores that carry my book, I would like to say thanks. I would also like to thank all my readers and supporters because without you I wouldn't have a writing career.

And last but not least, I can't go without sending a big shout-out to Keith of Marion Design for hooking up my cover and Tom from MK Group for his guidance through this whole publishing thing. Let's keep moving and make this thing happen on a grander scale.

Introduction

This book was probably the most challenging work that I have ever done. I struggled with many things while writing this book. I thought about how my Deacon father would react to the language used in this book. I thought about what my mother's reaction to the cover and content would be. I even thought about my friends and former students. Then I thought about it and I realized that I'm just a writer trying to convey a message to my readers.

I've even had to deal with the question whether or not I'm a freak from some of my friends after they read my first two books, Neglected Souls and Meeting Ms. Right. I keep telling them that writing is all about imagination, but they don't want to believe me. The sooner they realize that my imagination goes far beyond what they can see, the better our friendships will be. I never intended for my own personal sex life to be the dominating topics of our conversations. I guess sex just gets people riled up and talking, but they're not always talking about it when it's necessary.

We have allowed sex to become so taboo in our society, we sometimes think of it as despicable when someone uses certain terms to describe it, but sometimes it is what it is and we have to learn to accept that. My attempt in this book was to bring light to something that's very relevant in our community and society as a whole. Many people don't realize that sex is the most dangerous addiction and dependency that exist in our society.

Sex is really the root of all evil when placed in its proper context. Most people think they can use sex to get what they want in life. Some women think that their coochie is a prized possession and that they can use to control men whenever and however they want. Some men think their penis is a trophy and that they can use to manipulate women. I'm not saying that they're not prized possessions, but they're not always used for the betterment of mankind.

Most men seek wealth because their ultimate goal is to either impress women or get as many women as they can. Some men with wealth would buy as many as ten cars in an attempt to try to impress some needy and impressionable women. And we all know that only leads to one thing, sex. No man on earth without a family needs more than one car. Let's not even talk about the twenty room mansions that these men splurge on sometimes just to impress the opposite sex. But, it's not just the men because women do it too.

There are a lot of independent women out there who use their wealth to get what they want from men. A woman with money coupled with good looks is a deadly combination. Some men have fallen prey to these women and most of the time many of them can't handle it. However, many of them are foolish enough to believe that their good sex is what keeps these independent women around. Think again, buddy!

No matter how we try to downplay the role of sex, it is a vital part of our being. Human existence on earth would cease without sex. We need to be more open minded about sex so that we can help educate the younger generation about sexually transmitted diseases and the impact that sex can have on their lives. Sex is a powerful tool that can destroy a person's life as well as bring joy to a person. Most babies are born out of sex, not love. How will we start this open discussion about sex? I don't know because everyone is too embarrassed to discuss it. For now, let's start to open the communication lines by enjoying the book that I've written about a woman who allowed sex and control to take over her life.

Chapter 1

It had been a while since Darren was so ferocious with me in the bedroom. I had been yearning for his touch and he had been avoiding making love to me ever since I brought up the fact that I wanted to work on myself before I totally committed to him. Darren loves me and he tries as much as he can to fulfill my uncontrollable sexual desires and appetite, but every man has his limits. As much as Darren loves me, he is not ready to watch another man stick his dick in my mouth while he fucks me from behind. Over the years, we had done a lot of crazy shit sexually, but the one fantasy that I really wanted to live out was to have Darren and another man fuck me at the same time, and I knew it would remain a fantasy for the rest of my life. There was no way that Darren would allow another man to fuck his woman while he's in the room.

Darren has never lost his passion for me even though I have put him through the fire. I guess he spoiled me and drove me to the point where there was no end to my needs. If I had never developed a sexual obsession and dependency, I would have never run through so many men and women. But tonight, Darren is just enough for me. I don't know where he gets his energy from because we have been going at it for the last couple of hours. I must have climaxed at least five or six times already. The only thing that's bothering me right now is that I'm a little sore from all the thrusting and banging that he's been doing to my pussy all night. He only came once since we've been going at it.

I hope he's not trying to prove to me that he's all that I need sexually. Darren should know by now that he's all that I need to be sexually satisfied. As good as he is in bed I don't think any other man could ever replace that part of him in me. I'll always use my vibrators and other sexual toys to fulfill my sexual needs when he's not around to please me, but I won't look for another man to fuck. The vibrating sensation of my Silver Bullet takes me to another place and I can't give that up, not even for Darren. I know that he gets mad sometimes because I'm sharing my pussy with a few toys, but I can't help it. If it were up to me, I would gladly let him fuck me every-day until I'm satisfied. Sometimes, it's just easier for me to work out my own orgasms. I understand that Darren is tired sometimes when he gets home from work, but sex five times a week just isn't enough for me. He just has to get used to the idea that I'm a sexual beast.

Darren never lost his sex appeal over the years and he continues to turn me on just as much as he did when we were in high school. Tonight, my plan was to make love to the sweet sound of Sade because it took so long for me to get Darren back into my life. But nature took its course and Darren had his own plans in the works for me. Darren fucked me so well I thought I was going to faint. The more he made me scream, the more aroused I became. However, tonight, I could tell that Darren wanted to make sure he wore my pussy out so I would never think about another man again. He wanted to teach me a lesson. He used his magic tongue and his even more magi-cal dick like a magic wand to make all my sexual dreams come true. I kept playing with my clit and sensually fondling my breasts because I knew it turned Darren on. But in a way, I think it just fueled him with energy because he was like a beast that I had never seen before.

I have to admit to myself that I'm really and truly in love with Darren. I don't want to be cured of my sexual addiction to him because I enjoy sex with him too much. Not all illness-es need to be cured. I'm glad that I met a man early in my life who has loved me unconditionally and who has allowed me to explore my own world and make my own mistakes before we settle down. Darren knows that I love him and he also knows that sometimes I may have more of a sexual appetite than he can handle. Now he knows for certain that I would never run out on him with anybody ever again. I couldn't live without him in my life.

Chapter 2

Most psychologists will have you believe that I was molested as a child because of my promiscuity. I happen to have an insatiable sexual appetite and because of that I'm always under the scrutiny of everyone's diagnosis. Some people label me a hoe, some people label me a bitch, some people label me a whore and some people would have the world believe that I'm a nymphomaniac. Maybe they're not all completely wrong, but who gave them the license to be my psychologist. There's no other feeling in the world that tops an orgasm. Sex is not just pleasure to me, it also relieves my tension and it's a necessity. If I don't have sex at least seven times a week, I'm not in a good mood.

I developed my sexual appetite very early in life. I happened to be one of those overly developed adolescents when I was in my pre-teens. I had boobs almost as big as my mother's and my ass was the perfect size of a well shaped onion. I can't recall what my exact measurements were, but I had grown-ass men whistling at me by the time I reached age twelve. As much as I would have liked to think of myself as a mature twelve year-old, after growing into adulthood I realized I was not mature at all. I stood about five feet four inches tall when I was just twelve years old and weighed about one hundred and twenty pounds. And the weight was evenly distributed to all the right places. My tities were a good thirty two D and the only reason I remember that was because my mom was always making a big deal of the fact that she had to buy me grown-up bras.

I remember at one point during my early teenage years I couldn't even walk to the store without a bunch of older men making lewd comments at me. These assholes acted like I couldn't hear them. If they knew what kind of man my daddy was, most of them wouldn't even look my way. Another thing, I just know that I love my daddy to death. He's the sweetest man on this planet and he has spoiled me to the point where sometimes I feel guilty if I ask him for anything. Even my older brother, Will, allows me to get away with murder and he's a big guy just like my daddy. Okay, my daddy is not just big, he's huge. He stands about six feet seven inches tall and weighs about two hundred and eighty pounds of muscle. He used to be a linebacker in college. When he hurt his knee his career came to an abrupt end. Sometimes, I feel like my daddy is trying to live his life vicariously through Will, who's now a professional football player in the NFL.

From the time we were five years old, my mother, Gail, would take me to my gymnastic classes while my daddy, Allen, took my brother to his Pop Warner football games. As we got older, my parents would switch roles and my mother became the loudest cheerleading Pop Warner mom on the field for Will. I have had some great times with my family and I love every single one of them. The only person I ever loved as much outside of my family is my boyfriend, Darren. However, before I even go into in-depth details about Darren, I have to finish telling you about my wonderful family.

When my brother and I were young, my mother stayed home to take care of us while my dad worked. And when we were old enough to attend school, she returned to work, but she had a flexible enough schedule where she could pick up my brother and I from school everyday and stay home with us until my dad got home. Since her husband was the boss, she had all the flexibility that she needed. My mother would make sure that our homework was done and that dinner was ready by the time daddy got home. He didn't always make it home on time for dinner and she would get angry with him sometimes. But for the most part, my mother was very forgiving when it came to my daddy. She was happy to have a nice home with two wonderful children, a loving husband and a nice Cadillac to drive. We are the Stevens family.

My father is what most people would refer to as a blue-collar worker. That's what he appears to be on the surface, anyway. My father hardly tells his personal business to people because he did not want them coming to him with their problems. His only concern was his family and he provided well for us. My dad actually owned the construction company that everyone thought he worked for. He wore a yellow hard hat, denim jeans and a denim shirt to work everyday while driving his company truck with the insignia Stevens' Son and Daughter Construction Company plastered on the doors and the back of the truck. No one knew what Stevens' Son and Daughter Construction stood for except for him and my mother. My daddy never even told me and my brother that he owned that construction company. When we were old enough to work, every year, he acted like he had to talk to his boss to get me and my brother jobs at his company for the summer. I guess that was his way of keeping us from getting too spoiled.

Most people consider my family to be attractive. My mother is a short and very attractive dark skinned woman with a body to die for. My father is light skinned and he is what I have heard most women refer to as handsome. Personally, I think my daddy is the bomb. He looks like a big tall Quincy Jones to me. I look more like mother, but my complexion is closer to my father's. My brother is the spitting image of my dad with a caramel complexion. When I'm with my mother, everyone thinks that we're sisters. And when I'm with my father, everyone thinks I look just like him. My brother and I share some physical features as well. We are one happy, good looking family.

My parents have been very close and happily married ever since I can remember. Don't get me wrong, they have had their quarrels as well, but it was the way that they made up that drew my interest when I was younger. After a big fight with my mother, my father would go out and get flowers, a card and a bottle of champagne and bring them back home to make up with her. And they didn't even keep what they were doing behind closed doors a secret from Will and me. My daddy would carry my mother upstairs to the bedroom and he would lock the door so my brother and I couldn't barge in on them. Within minutes, I would start hearing the moaning and groaning from my mother and my daddy screaming to her "Who's the man?" Then the moaning would stop and she would start screaming "give it to me, big daddy. It's yours, take it". That shit would go on and on and occasionally my mother would scream "I'm coming, oh God I'm coming".

After each of those sessions, my parents would be in a better mood and my brother and I could get anything we wanted out of them. We had our routine down pat. We would always wait until after my parents came out of the bedroom smiling and sweaty from all the banging they had just done and we'd ask them for money or toys or whatever it was that we wanted and they never said no. Seeing my mother so happy after a lovemaking session with my dad intensified my curiosity. I always wondered what he did to her that was so good that she didn't only forgive him, but as kids, we were able to get whatever we wanted from them as well.

When I was a kid, my daddy would always lock the door when he went in the shower and he would always come out wearing his towel around his waist on the way to the bedroom. Being the nosey little girl that I was, I would try to look through the key hole on the old door lock to see what my daddy was trying to keep hidden from me and my brother. That would mark the time that I became very curious about the human anatomy as a very young child. The more my father wrapped that towel around his waist, the more curious I became and the more determined I was about finding out what was underneath.

One day after my daddy walked out of the bathroom to go to his room, he forgot to lock the door behind him and I walked right in when he was getting dressed. It was the first time that I saw my daddy naked. I knew that I shouldn't have opened the door on him, but I did it because I was curious. I saw his four inch limped penis dangling as he put on his underwear. He immediately ordered me out of the room, so he could finish getting dressed. It wasn't until years later when I became an adult that I realized that my daddy had a huge penis to go with his huge body. As an adult, I learned that the average size penis is between one and a half to two and half inches when it's soft. That meant that my daddy was packing at least ten inches when he was erected. No wonder my mom was always screaming.

My very first sight of a penis was my daddy's and I was just seven years old. Even then, I felt that what I was doing was naughty. That was also the last time I ever walked in on my father while he was getting dressed. There were other times when I barged into my parents' room without knocking as well, but they were never doing anything. However, there was this one particular time when I walked in on them and my dad scolded me like he had never done in his life. When I walked in on my parents that particular day, I found my father sitting on the edge of the bed with his legs wide open and my mother kneeling in front of him butt naked holding his huge dick in her hands like it was a giant ice cream cone and she was licking the head like it was about to spill over. My dad had his head tilted back while he enjoyed the soothing touch of my mother's tongue around his penis. My mother was more than happy to get her palms around his dick stroking it back and forth as she licked it. The joy that dick brought to her face made me wonder if it was tasty.

I had never seen my daddy so angry after I entered the room. I must've interrupted his trip to seventh heaven. He grabbed one of the pillows and he held it in front of him while he chased me out of the room. He told me that he was going to punish me for walking into the room without knocking and for also leaving my brother's side in the game room. My mother wasn't as angry as he was because she figured that I wouldn't have been able to interpret what I had seen. I dashed out of the room and ran back to be by Will's side in the game room.

My dad always left strict instructions not to leave the game room when he and my mom were upstairs getting it on. Even though he was mad at me for walking in on him, that didn't stop him from going ahead with his plans to have my mother scream his name and the Lord's name in vain while he pleased her moments later. And by the time he was done with her, he had completely forgotten what I had done. My parents were just different creatures after sex and I couldn't wait to find out what was so good about sex that altered my parents' mood so frequently.

As I started getting older, the vivid pictures of what I saw in my parents' room stayed on my mind and I wanted to know what they were doing. Although the moaning and groaning was substantially lessened as my brother and I got older, we could still hear the banging of the headboard, sometimes. One day I brought everything that I saw as a child back to my mother and surprisingly, she did not hide anything from me. From the time I was twelve years old, my mother was very open with me and she talked to me about sex and told me that it was not a dirty thing to do if I wanted to do it when I got older. While my mother schooled me in her own way, my father schooled my brother in a totally different way. It was okay for my brother to start experimenting when he was very young.

My parents didn't allow me to date until I was sixteen years old, but my brother had a girlfriend when he was just fifteen. My dad had a double standard and my mom just went along with whatever he said. But it would be my brother that would raise my curiosity in sex to the point where I wanted to have my first encounter. He had this girlfriend that he used to sneak into the basement while my mother was upstairs watching television. And every time they went downstairs, she would give him what I later found out were blowjobs, until he couldn't take it anymore. I used to peep through the key hole to see my brother's body trembling every time he was coming and his girlfriend used to take it down her throat like a champ. I never once saw her spit out anything. The more I watched them, the more I wanted to try it out for myself. What was even more intriguing to me was the fact that my brother's girlfriend was able to get anything out of him after giving him a blowjob. He would buy her whatever she wanted with his allowance.

Chapter 3

As much trash as the kids around the school were talking about the girls who sucked dicks, I didn't care about what they said. I couldn't wait to get on my knees to start sucking the biggest dick I could find and have the boy succumb to my sexual prowess. I'm not saying that I was an expert just yet, but I had watched my brother's girlfriend enough times to know that keeping my teeth out of the way was essential to a good blowjob. I would hear my brother whisper to her "No teeth. Just use your tongue like you're sucking on a lollipop". She would follow my brother's instructions and over time she became a pro at it. I was also practicing my own craft as I watched my brother and his girlfriend. I started bringing a cucumber with me to the key hole every time I went down to watch them.

Whenever my brother came home from football practice, he would jump in the shower then tell my mother that he was going downstairs to study because of the peace and quiet in the back room in the basement. I knew whenever he said that, his girlfriend was waiting out back for him to open the basement door so she could get in. I would always give them a ten minute headstart before I went downstairs to watch them. That Negro knew damn well that the quietest place in the house was his bedroom if he really wanted to study, but for some reason, my mother bought his story. He would always have his girlfriend out of the house by the time my dad got home. My daddy was too smart for his tricks.

After watching my brother ejaculate about a dumpster's worth of semen down his girlfriend's throat over a period of a year, I was ready to start my on intake of semen. I had been practicing sucking with a cucumber for the last year and I was

11

ready to get started with the real thing. The only problem was that my parents didn't allow me to go anywhere for too long by myself. They were like watchdogs. They made sure they knew our whereabouts all the time. My brother had managed to get his groove on because his girlfriend had a lot more freedom than we did. For me, getting away from my parents was the biggest problem.

I wasn't worried about finding a boy who wanted me to suck his dick. I was attractive enough for most of the boys at the high school to try to get with me, but they were all afraid of my brother and even more afraid of my dad. My dad made sure that everyone at the school knew who he was and who his children were. He used to stop by the school on his way to work just to check on our progress. Even though my mother was at the school all the time, he made sure that he let the staff at the school know that he was also involved. The name Mr. Stevens had a familiar ring with all my teachers and he made sure that everyone knew my name, Tina Stevens.

My dad also made sure that the boys at the school knew that he wasn't anything to mess with and he would kill anyone who touched his little girl. Sometimes he would go up to the school unannounced and would call on the boys that looked most like players and ask them, "Have you seen my daughter, Tina?" in the most intimidating tone. The boys would come back to me and tell me how they were horrified of my dad. He was indeed very intimidating in size, but he looked even more frightening in his work clothes. For some reason, construction workers seem to have that rough and rugged tough look that instills fear in a lot of people. And my father didn't need to be in his construction clothes to instill fear. Even when he wore his business suits, the staff at the school was afraid of him.

At least my parents didn't have to worry about the school system where we lived like most of the members of the rest of our family whose children lived in New York City and attended the New York City Public Schools. We lived in the

Suffolk County part of Long Island where my parents got the most out of their tax dollars. The school system in Long Island was much better than New York City and my parents didn't have to waste their hard earned money on private schools for Will and I. The teachers at the school earned enough money to make sure that they did their jobs well. Also, the requirements to become a teacher in Long Island were a lot higher than the New York City public school system.

Chapter 4

My big dilemma was that I wanted to start getting hands-on practice to improve my oral skills, but I couldn't get away from my parents. Even worse, was the fact that if they knew that I was about to become sexually active at the age of fourteen they would either kill me or lock me downstairs in the basement until I became a grown woman. My sexual interest peaked by accident. I was in the shower one day washing myself and I felt this sensation throughout my body when the water pressure hit my clit. It was a feeling that I had never felt before. The water stimulated me in ways that I wanted to indulge in. After that first experience, I found myself taking long hot showers and masturbating and reaching orgasms every morning, noon and night. Then I started using my fingers to masturbate in my bedroom with my door locked. The more I masturbated, the more I enjoyed it. When my fingers got tired, I used a cucumber that was almost seven inches in length and very thick in width to satisfy my needs. To be honest, I think I popped my own cherry with a cucumber when I was fourteen years old.

Even my nipples would sometimes get hard in the shower from the water pressure. I used every type of stimulation system to get off. I became this little horny toad who couldn't get enough sex by the age of fourteen. Playing with myself and satisfying my needs was one thing, however, I still yearned to satisfy a boy with what I thought were my polished devilish oral skills. I wanted to use my sexual skills to control the boys at my school, church, playground and anywhere there were boys. If my parents were even aware of my daily thoughts, I would have been sent to a convent.

The only two penises that I had ever seen were my father's and Will's when I was being nosey and to me they were pretty huge. So, I used their size as the measuring requirement for a good size dick. My mother was always satisfied with my father and Will's girlfriend came over almost everyday to get fucked by him. I learned very early on that size mattered a lot. Any guy whose dick I was going to suck would at least have to be able to stand up to my seven-inch requirement. I used to hear the saying "size doesn't matter and that it's the motion of the ocean" from people all the time, but I was always quick to tell them to stop fooling themselves. I felt that women who said that were just afraid to say that they wanted a big dick for fear that they would be labeled a ho by other people. If I could write a song about loving a big dick, I would. That's why I love the sexual freedom that Li'l Kim brought to Hip Hop in the mid-nineties. Where was she when I was fourteen? She had to come out after I became an adult. However, I would be proven wrong later on in my life by a man who only had a six-inch dick.

The restrictions my parents placed on me, forced me to try to fulfill my sexual desires in the nastiest places when I was younger. The first time I attempted to suck somebody's dick was in the bathroom at my high school. This very handsome boy and I made plans to ask our teachers for a pass to the bathroom at eleven o'clock in the morning during third period. We met in the hallway and we walked downstairs to the staff bathroom and locked the door. I pulled down his pants and I almost laugh when I saw his little tiny dick. I was even willing to completely forgo my requirement of seven inches because I wanted to finally taste a real dick. I took his dick in my hand and started stroking it back and forth the same way I had watched my brother's girlfriend do it to him. I did it to the point where he couldn't stand it anymore and before I could even put his little dick in my mouth, this mother fucker came all over himself. I was so pissed and I told him that if he told anybody that I gave him a hand job, I would not only tell them that he came in thirty seconds, but I would also get my brother to kick his ass.

I then realized that the pretty boys and the guys that all the women lusted after didn't necessarily pack the kind of meat that I was interested in. I had gotten almost all the cute boys at my school to go with me to the staff bathroom that year and I never got a chance to suck any of their dicks because most of them came by the time I reached out to grab their dicks. Half of those pretty and popular boys were a big disappointment. It was time for me to move on to older folks because these young boys disappointed me for the whole school year.

I continued to masturbate that whole summer and I think I was able to totally master the art of masturbation by the time I turned fifteen. I came when and how I wanted using whatever tool or technique that I wanted. It was hard for me to do anything with any guys because my mother spent most of her time with me and Will during the summer doing a lot of stupid activities. Since we were one of only two black families on our street, I didn't have any black boys to "play" with. My brother was lucky however, because the other black couple who lived on our street had three daughters. I was always envious of him because I knew he was sleeping with two of the sisters. My brother was a dog. He was able to sneak these girls in the basement without my mother knowing. Whenever my brother wanted to get away from my mother to go fuck one of the sisters, he acted like he wanted to go to the basement to read a book. And I was not allowed to go with him because he needed peace and quiet.

While my brother was improving his sexual skills with the neighbors' daughters, I was watching their every move and learning every trick from them. My brother was a beast who was able to fuck these girls three to four times a day when he was about seventeen years old. One time he even talked them into having a three-some with him, but one of the sisters got jealous when he was giving more attention to the prettier sister with the bigger butt. He was fucking the prettier one with the bigger butt longer than the other one. I heard them tell him that they would never do a three-some with him again. I don't know where my brother learned to fuck the way he did, but he was good. I don't know if my dad used to tell him what to do or if they discussed it, but he was damn good.

Chapter 5

When I returned to school that fall, I was a horny fifteen year-old sophomore looking to suck a few good dicks and getting my pussy sucked by a few good looking upper classmen in the process. I didn't think I was ready to get fucked by anybody just yet. My cucumbers were good enough as far as penetration. I used to fuck the hell out of my cucumbers. I didn't want to be around the boys my age anymore because they had no dick control and their dicks were small. Out of all those boys that I toyed around with, in the bathroom during my freshman year in high school, only one had a five-inch dick. The others didn't even come close. I would guess their dicks still needed time to mature. I knew that the seventeen year-old guys would have developed more than the fourteen year olds and they would have a better idea about what to do to please me as well as controlling their premature ejaculation.

Even though my parents forbade me to date until I was sixteen years old, my mother still allowed me to buy some sexy outfits for the school year. It was the fall of 1990 when I entered my sophomore year in high school. I bought a lot tight fitted jeans, mini skirts and spandex shorts. On the first day of school, I wore these tight jeans that I damn near sweat a bucket to force myself into. My ass was looking juicy and plumped and I couldn't wait for the older guys to take notice. I also wore a tight little sweater that accentuated my D cup breasts and I knew that nobody was going to be able to avoid my knockers.

As fine as I thought I looked, my daddy was about to throw a monkey wrench in my game. When I looked outside and saw his truck idling in the driveway, I knew that he was going to be the one to drive me to school on the first day of school like he had done for the last ten years. I was crossing my fingers and hoping he wouldn't say anything about my outfit and just like that, when I got downstairs, he sent me back upstairs to change. I had to appease to my mother's fashion sense in order to convince her to let me wear my outfit to school. She pleaded with him and told him that I was growing as a woman and I needed to start developing some kind of fashion sense and that there was nothing wrong with what I was wearing. My father told her that he didn't want any boys coming around the house until I was at least sixteen years old and nothing would change that. My mother assured him that I was under her watchful eye from the time school let out and that he had nothing to worry about. Boy! They couldn't be more wrong.

Being under what my mother believed to be her guise all the time, forced me to be more creative and evasive. Since school was the only place that I could really be free, I decided that I was also going to be as freaky as I wanted to be there as well. The first thing I learned in high school was that the teachers did not want to be parents. They simply wanted to come to the school to teach then go about their day. Even the principal at my school was too busy to monitor the five hundred student population at my school. Making things easier for me was the fact that we didn't have any hall monitors. The school departments in suburbia didn't see any threats from their pupils that would warrant spending extra money on hall monitors.

When I arrived at school on my first day, my dad walked me through the hall to pick up my new schedule and he made sure he met every single one of my teachers, while he allowed my brother who was a senior to run off and do his own thing. He gave his personal phone number to all the teachers in case I ever act up in school. My dad also tried as much as he could to intimidate every guy he thought looked like a player, with his nasty and deadly stares. It was his way of marking his territory and the guys took notice almost immediately when they saw this huge man escorting me through the hallway.

My dad finally left the school and I reported to my first period class, but the whole time while I was walking with my dad down the hallway, I noticed this beautiful god of a boy looking at me and smiling. I later found out that his name was Chris and he was a senior who had just transferred from Stuyvesant High School in Brooklyn. His parents moved during his last year of school because he was starting to get out of hand and they wanted to make sure that he didn't mess up his chances of going to a good college. Chris was the only guy who didn't seem intimidated by my dad. He was about six feet two inches tall with an athletic build. He was a football and basketball standout back in his old high school. I could tell that all the girls at the school were going to be jocking him, but I had to get to him first. I always found a way to get what I wanted.

Chapter 6

The whole time I was in class, I was thinking about how I was gonna take Chris to the teachers' bathroom in the basement and suck the hell out of his dick. And that moment would soon arrive. The bell finally rang and I woke out of my dream state. When I walked out into the hall way, I found Chris leaning against the wall and smiling at me from ear to ear. He told me that he had followed me to class from a distance and he wanted to make sure that his face was the first thing I saw when I came out of class. His game was already better than all the other corny guys that I talked to in the past and I was thinking that this guy didn't even know that I had planned to swallow him whole by the end of the school day.

Chris and I got to talk a little and I found out that he wasn't just a smooth talker, but he was also a bad boy from Brooklyn who enjoyed a challenge. Little did he know, I was not gonna be that much of a challenge at all. I had already given in to him when I saw his beautiful smile when I came out of the classroom. Chris was very good looking, dark and talked the kind of slang that only a Brooklynite could speak. I made plans with Chris to meet in the hall down the basement during fifth period at 12:30 PM, so we could take a trip down to the bathroom. I was in class anxiously waiting for the clock to hit 12:29 so I could ask my teacher for a pass to the bathroom. My mind was everywhere except where it needed to be, in class listening to the teacher's lesson plan. I got my pass and finally the time had arrived for me to go meet with Chris.

I was skipping down the hallway like Annie Hall and when Chris came around the corner and grabbed hold of my hand, I almost melted. I led him straight to the teachers' bathroom and I locked the door. He pulled me towards him and he started kissing me softly around my neck, my chin and then finally he kissed my lips. I went for the gusto, though. I stuck my tongue inside his mouth and before I knew it we were both breathing heavy and I didn't want him to stop kissing me. I was enjoying his kisses so much that I didn't even get a chance to pull his dick out of his pants. However, his dick was hard enough that when he was grinding on me while we were kissing, I knew he had to be packing at least seven inches. I took a look at my watch and I noticed we had about five minutes left before the bell rang, so I fixed my hair and came out the bathroom first and then he followed. I ran back to my class holding my stomach, acting like it was that time of the month so my male teacher would be sympathetic and not scold me for having been gone for fifteen minutes. I knew a lot of tricks. Whenever I took a long time to return to class, I acted like I had my period and no teacher wants to address a student's menstrual cramps in front of the class.

A part of me was disappointed that I didn't get to suck Chris's dick in the bathroom, but it all worked out for the better. I also learned that Chris had a car that his parents bought him during his last year of school and both his parents worked in Manhattan and no one was home during the day. I couldn't talk to Chris on the phone because my parents didn't allow me to speak to boys. I tried to get as much information as possible from Chris during school. We made plans to meet in the bathroom again the following day, but this time it would be during third period. All the other girls in the school noticed that I was talking to Chris and they all became jealous of me. The young boys whose dick that I played with the year before were looking at me funny too, but they couldn't dare say anything about me because they knew that my brother would kick their ass. None of those chumps were tough enough to stand up to my brother and the idea of having to face my father would send them shitting in their pants.

I had to also warn Chris that we had to keep our little interludes a secret from my brother because I didn't want it to get back to my dad. My daddy had never raised his hands to me, but I didn't want to find out what they felt like either. Chris was aware of my brother, but he didn't seem like he was shaking in his pants. He had this casual arrogance about him that made him so sexy to me. He didn't even call me by my full name, Tina, he simply called me T. It must've been a Brooklyn thing. I grew up in Long Island all my life, so I was not accustomed to the Brooklyn ways, but I loved it.

When the time arrived to meet Chris during third period, I held on to my stomach like I had cramps and my female teacher sympathized with me and told me to take all the time that I needed before I returned to class. I didn't know how Chris was able to stay out of class for so long, but I guess he didn't really care. We went to the bathroom and continued with our kissing again. The last time, I was so anxious, I didn't even realized how soft and moist Chris's lips were. His tongue was also smooth and his breath was very fresh from the Spearmint gum that he was chewing.

While he wanted to kiss me a little bit longer, I wanted to taste his dick in my mouth. I unzipped his pants, pulled out his dick and I started playing with it. I kept stroking it while we kissed and he didn't succumb to the touch of my hands like the other preemies who wasted my time in the previous year. Then finally, I bent down and wrapped my mouth around his dick which was maybe six and a half inches long. He was about half an inch short of my requirement, but I didn't care.

I started sucking his dick and watching his face to see his reaction. I twirled my tongue around the tip then forcefully suck on it like I was trying to squeeze the last drop from the plastic wrap of an icy. I noticed that every time I took his whole dick into my mouth he would close his eyes like he was about to cum and I wanted him to cum before the bell rang. With the warmth of my mouth wrapped around his dick and my tongue circling it, he screamed that he was coming and I quickly pulled his dick out of my mouth to squeeze every little bit of his juice out with my hand. After he was done, he zipped up his pants and gave me one last kiss before I went to class.

Chris and I continued to have our little interludes in the bathroom for a couple of weeks and I was getting bored and tired of sucking his dick. I wanted him to start eating my pussy. I wasn't ready to get fucked by him yet, though. I kept turning him down every time he tried to stick his dick inside of me. And the stupid boy didn't even have a condom. I found out that Chris wasn't as bright as I thought. I kept turning him down for pussy because he never had a condom and not once did the boy think about bringing a condom to the bathroom with him. I was not going to take any chances with him and have my daddy beat my ass for getting pregnant. At least, he would have stood a chance of getting some pussy if he was smart enough to bring a condom with him just once. Lord knows what I would have done in the heat of the moment.

Anyway, my afternoon rendezvous in the bathroom with Chris ended when he continued to refuse to eat my pussy. The blowjob sessions all came to an abrupt end and I was not interested in him anymore. That mother fucker had the nerve to tell me that "I don't eat pussy. Only punk ass dudes eat pussy". I'm glad that Li'l Kim made pussy eating a fashionable thing for men to do in some of her songs during the late nineties because a lot of sisters suffered before she stepped on the scene. Say what you will about Li'l Kim, but she served a purpose.

Since Chris didn't want to eat my pussy, I had to find a guy who did and I made a promise to myself that I was not gonna suck anybody's dick unless they ate my pussy first, back in high school. Chris missed out on a lot just because he refused to eat my pussy. I had planned on sucking his dick in his car, doing shit to him that he had never imagined, but it was his loss. However, I went back on the promise of not sucking any guy unless they went down on me first, many times. I have since sucked so many dicks without waiting for the guys to eat my pussy that I can't even keep count. I just have a weakness for a nice size looking dick. Every time I saw a satisfying looking dick I had to suck it. A good dick was like kryptonite to me.

Most women who suck dick won't admit that they enjoy doing it. Well, I'm not one of them. During the last couple of years of high school I went back to my requirement of everyone pleasing me first before I pleased them and it only happened with four guys. And none of them ate my pussy as well as I sucked their dicks. I never even came while they were eating me. I had those weak links' bodies jerking and screaming for mercy in the bathroom. I never allowed any of those guys in high school to sleep with me. I was still a virgin as far as I was concerned. It wasn't until after I met my boyfriend, Darren, that I started having sex during my last year in high school.

Chapter 7

Darren was a sweetheart that I met during my senior year at the school. He was on the wrestling team and everybody knew that he was like a quiet storm. One of the reasons why I liked Darren so much was because he had kicked Chris's ass when Chris came out of his face to call me a bitch during Darren's junior year and Chris' second year as a senior at the high school. His dumb ass was held back because he had failed every single one of his classes. I also found out that Chris only sported a tough guy image to impress people. He was never really that tough. He waited until after my brother graduated from the school to start disrespecting me. But who knew he had it coming from Darren.

Chris got his ass whipped by Darren in the school yard. His bitch ass didn't even know how to fight and everyone at the school stopped buying into his Brooklyn tough guy image. Darren actually grew up in Jamaica, Queens, but his parents moved to Long Island when he was a freshman in high school. He wasn't the tallest guy that I ever dated, but he was built like Mike Tyson. Daren was about five feet nine inches tall and weighed about one hundred and ninety pounds of solid muscle. He was also the captain of the wrestling team.

Chris thought he could intimidate Darren because he towered over him in height and he was considerably bigger than Darren as he had grown to be six feet seven inches tall and weighed about two hundred and sixty pounds easily during his second year as a senior at the high school. But they say "The bigger they come, the harder the fall". And that's exactly what happened to Chris when Darren met him in the school yard for a fight. Darren dropped his ass to the ground with one punch. The whole thing initially started when Chris called me a bitch. Darren told him that it was disrespectful for any man to call a woman a bitch, especially a black woman. Chris turned to him and said, "Your mother's a bitch too, chump". Darren wanted to break his neck right away when he said that, but he didn't want to fight him in the school. Instead, he asked Chris to show how tough he really was after school in the yard. I felt bad for Chris because he never even stood a chance against Darren. He must've thrown about four punches at Darren, which none ever connected. Darren connected to his jaw with the first punch and the lights were out for him. He ended up dropping out of school after that incident because he was no longer the tough guy from Brooklyn.

Darren looked so sexy defending me that day. His bulging muscles and gentleness had my pussy wet from the time he told Chris not to call me a bitch. Darren did not have a rugged exterior like most of the boys at the school tried to carry. He was clean cut, respectful, studious and well behaved all the time. He worked out relentlessly in the gym and was on his way to attend Syracuse University on a full academic scholarship the upcoming fall. He and I had never spoken prior to the incident. By the time I became a senior in high school, I was allowed to date openly by my parents. My mom no longer picked me up from school and I had my own car as well. I offered to drive Darren home after the fight and we ended up taking a detour to one of the local parks. Darren and I sat in the park and talked for almost two hours, by the time I realized that much time had gone by, I was mesmerized by him. I told him that I had to get home as I hurried to drop him off at home. We exchanged phone numbers and he promised to call me later that evening.

When I got home, I lied to my mother and told her that I went to the library to research a term paper that I was doing for my history class. I tried to get through my homework as fast as I could because my parents didn't allow me to get on the phone until after my homework was done and I was expecting Darren to call me. I finished my homework in no time and afterwards, I went to my room to play with myself until Darren called. I had my music blasted to draw out the moaning and groaning sound I was making while fingering myself and rubbing my clit until I came over and over. I even took out a cucumber from the fridge and I imagined it was Darren's dick while I sat in my room and sucked on it. I couldn't wait to get my hands on the real thing. Even though Darren was a little shy, I knew he could handle himself in the bedroom because of the way he took care of Chris.

Darren finally called me around nine o'clock that night and I only had one hour to talk to him. My parents didn't allow us to stay on the phone after ten o'clock on a school night. My parents were very strict and the stricter they were with me, the more I tried to get away with mischievous behavior. Darren and I picked up from where we left off in the park and I wanted to introduce him to my special place at the school the following day. We made plans to meet in the hallway down in the basement during third period. I didn't give Darren any reason for the meeting. I simply told him to meet me and that I would have a surprise for him. I had no idea that Darren would have a surprise for me.

I used the same old tricks that I had been using in the past to get a pass from my teacher to go meet with Darren. I met Darren in the basement as planned then I grabbed his hands and told him to follow me. I took him into the teachers' bathroom. After we closed the door behind us, Darren grabbed me and pulled me towards him and started tonguing me. He was very different from the other guys that I had been with. This quiet, shy guy was passionate and had the kind of aggression that I had been yearning for since I started high school. I could see the bulge in his pants and it was very unusual.

Darren picked me up and had my feet suspended up in the air as he continued to kiss me and making his way down my blouse to my chest. His tongue was wandering my body like a river overriding its dam and I enjoyed every minute of it. The movements of Darren's tongue made me wonder if he could use it on my pussy to make me cum like I had never cum in my life. And before I could say anything, Darren lifted my skirt up and pulled my underwear to the side and started giving me the tongue treatment that I had been yearning for. He ate my pussy like he was a professional porn star giving an Oscar performance in front of a camera. He made me believe that he was the best pussy eater that ever lived and to confirm it, I came at least three times. I didn't even get a chance to play with his dick. By the time I came the third time, I was almost too weak to walk back to class. Darren told me that he had to return to class but we would finish it on Friday when I see him for our first date.

Chapter 8

After that day, I knew that Darren wasn't the type of guy that I wanted to be with in a small cramped bathroom. I needed to be in a big room where I could move around freely with him. I knew that Darren was gonna be rocking my world and I was getting my pussy ready to get torn up on Friday. I drove Darren home after school that day and all I could think about was him tearing my pussy to pieces. I couldn't wait to ride him and kiss his rippled body all over and lick his dick like he had never been licked before. Darren had put it on me and I couldn't wait to return the favor. I felt like I had to prove myself to him.

Friday finally came and Darren's parents drove down to Maryland for a weekend getaway. His parents trusted him as he had proven to them time and time again that he was a responsible young adult who could be trusted. After all, he was a straight "A" student, an athlete and a very likable young man. I arrived at Darren's house at seven thirty in the evening to pick him up for the eight o'clock show at the movie theatre and the first thing I noticed was that his parents' car was gone. After he got in the car, I asked him if his parents went out, he told me they went away for the weekend. I suggested nonchalantly to him to forgo the movie and stay home with him. He was more than happy with my suggestions. The minute I set foot in the house after closing the door behind us, I pulled Darren towards me and I almost ripped off his Polo shirt. I pushed him down on the staircase in the foyer leading to the second floor and I started kissing his chest and rubbing his nipples with my hands as he sat back enjoying it.

I maneuvered my tongue over to his left nipple and I started sucking on it and lightly biting it to get a reaction from him. He was moaning and I moved over to the right one and did the same thing. While I was trying to caress his chest with my mouth, he was trying to pull my sweater over my head to get to my double D cups. By the time I became a senior in high school my breasts had grown to a DD. He was playing with my nipples through my bra as I continued to suck on his nipple. I wanted to feel his soft lips against mine, so I reached for the back of his head and pulled him forcefully towards me and stuck my tongue in his mouth for him to suck on. While he was sucking on my tongue, I unclasped my bra to expose my huge tities into his hands. He caressed my tities with his hands while we pulled and sucked back and forth on each other's tongues. I could tell that he wanted to have my tities in his mouth, so I moved up to allow him to bring my tities together so he could suck on both nipples at the same time. He had a mouth full of tits and I was relishing in the orgasmic feeling that he was unleashing on me as his hands wandered into my pants down to my clit.

Darren sucked my breasts and rubbed my clit until I was forced to stop so I could get out of my pants. After my pants came off, I was standing in the foyer at his house in my underwear with my tities exposed and my nipples sticking up like icebergs. Darren was sitting on the stairs with his back leaning upward. I wanted to do something that would drive him wild, so I started sucking on my nipples and pulling on them as he watched me and smiled. I turned to shake my ass and acted like I was about to pull my underwear off to give him a quick glance at my wet pussy. I was trying to do a strip tease, but the only piece of clothing I had on was my underwear. It was enough with the teasing already! I wanted to get on my knees and start sucking his dick. Before I could pull off his pants, he grabbed my hand and led me to his bedroom upstairs. He laid down across his queen size bed with his feet hanging on the front of the bed and told me to pull his pants off.

As I started to pull off his pants, I noticed that he went totally commando on me. Darren was not wearing underwear. He had intended to fuck me after the movie all along. I was able to get his pants barely pass his thigh before I grabbed his twelve inch dick and wrapped my mouth around it. I could be very impatient when I see a nice dick and Darren had a nice one. He was even bigger than my brother. My cucumbers looked small compared to Darren's dick. I held his dick with both of my hands as I went up and down and across it with my tongue and softly blowing on it causing a sensation that drove Darren wild. I was glad to suck his dick and enjoyed holding it in my hands. I wanted to lick every popping vein and every contour line up and down his dick. Darren could tell that I was admiring his dick, so he sat back and allowed me to please him until he couldn't take it anymore. As nasty as the girls at my school made it sound to swallow, I took Darren's semen down my throat and squeezed his dick to savor every last drop that came out.

At seventeen years old, Darren didn't even lose his erection after he came. He pulled me up towards him for a kiss as I mounted him like a horse on the edge of the bed to get every single inch of his dick inside my hot pussy. Darren was hitting my sugar walls almost instantly and I could feel that I was about to reach an orgasm of magnitude proportion. I braced myself for his hard strokes as cum shot out of my pussy and down Darren's leg like we were on a dairy farm. He held on to my ass as he picked me up and brought me against the wall where he started banging me with all his strength. I was holding on to his neck for dear life and Darren was sweating bullets as he fucked the shit out of me for the next thirty minutes. By the time he came again, I had come twenty times over and my pussy was worn out. I knew that I had met my match and Darren was going to be in my life for a long time if I had anything to do with it.

Chapter 9

I completed the school year without embarrassing myself or Darren. He was the only guy that I ever saw in the teachers' bathroom for the rest of the year. However, as good as Darren was with his tool, it still wasn't enough to satisfy my sexual appetite. I was able to get a friend of mine who was eighteen years old to buy me a dildo at a sex shop in the Village while we were shopping in Manhattan. I bought a big one too. It was at least the size of Darren's dick or maybe even slightly bigger. That dildo became my best friend at night when I didn't have Darren to tear my pussy to pieces. I used to spread my leg open across my bed and pretended that Darren was in front of me with his big, rock hard dick standing straight up in my face. I would hold my dildo the same way I would hold on to Darren's dick and I did tricks to it with my tongue, my hands, and my mouth until I was satisfied. I even tried to deep throat my dildo the same way I attempted to deep throat Darren's dick once and almost choked on it. Swallowing his whole dick in my mouth was my biggest challenge and I was out to conquer it.

With much practice in my room with the dildo, I was able to swallow a good ten inches of it and each time I got with Darren, he noticed that I was taking in more of him in my mouth and for some reason that shit got him more excited. There was one time when I had him in my mouth and as I started to glide my way down almost to the bottom of his dick, he exploded in the back of my throat and I almost vomited all over him. Darren got off on shit that was out of the ordinary. Whenever Darren was about to come, he would bang me as hard as he could and his strokes would sometimes send the tip of his dick up to my pelvis and the shit would hurt. I tried using the dildo to get my pussy acclimated to his size and roughness, but I could never stick it in my pussy as hard as Darren would hump me. There were times when I asked Darren to fuck me hard because I was in the mood for rough sex, but I would always bleed afterwards.

Darren also had a knack and a gift to find my g-spot. I think he got me addicted to sex even more than I already was. I had gotten used to his touches, his kisses, his dick, his attitude and his ways. I spent the whole summer alongside Darren after we graduated from high school. We were like Bonnie and Clyde and we fucked all over the city and in every park that summer.

So, watching Darren's parents pack the car to take him to Syracuse for his freshman year at the University in September made me sad. My dick supply was moving about six hours away from me and I knew it was gonna be hard to find another guy to satisfy me the way Darren did. I was leaving for college myself at Mount Holyoke in Massachusetts in couple of days, but I wanted to take Darren's dick with me to my campus so I could have him all the time. I don't know if I was in love with Darren or if I just lusted after his big dick, but I wanted him near me. We had decided that the best thing to do was to date openly so that a long distance relationship wouldn't interfere with our studies. I could only imagine all the girls at Syracuse University waiting in line to get served by him.

I knew it was a matter of time before he slept with the first girl on campus, and she'd run around telling everybody how good his dick was and he would become the dick supplier for the whole campus. Women can never keep a good thing to themselves, especially good dick. I was sad to part from Darren, but there was a whole new world out there in western Massachusetts waiting to be conquered by me.

Chapter 10

When I first arrived on campus, I befriended this lesbian girl named Tanya. She came right out and told me that she was a lesbian. I was a little surprised that she was so open with her sexuality. I guess she didn't want any hang ups, gossips and rumors interrupting the friendship that we were about to develop. I heard it straight from the horse's mouth and she wasn't afraid to tell me.

Tanya was a gorgeous Puerto Rican girl from Springfield, Massachusetts and I could tell that she knew that she had it going on. She helped me unpack my belongings and arrange my room to my liking. By the time we were done, we were both hungry and it was time for dinner. We both went down to the school's cafeteria to eat dinner. While we were in the cafeteria, I told Tanya how excited I was about meeting my new roommate and wondered what she would be like.

I knew that my roommate was Caucasian from the information that I received in the mail about her during the summer from the school. She was into Hip Hop just like I was and she came from Cambridge, Massachusetts, which I heard was very diverse. I hoped that eventually my roommate, Tanya and I would become the three musketeers. After we were done eating dinner, I went back to my room and there was still no sign of my roommate. I went down the hall to Tanya's room to listen to music and wait for my roommate to show up. Tanya and I were engaged in a sexual conversation that was so deep and profound that we didn't even realize that it was ten thirty when we walked out of her room to go check if my roommate had arrived.

Tanya told me about her sexual escapades with other women and I have to admit that I was intrigued right away. She started telling me about the sensuality that she experienced at the touch of a woman's hand and that she didn't enjoy a man poking her from behind or sticking his dick inside of her. The thought of being with a man was nasty to Tanya. She knew that she was gay from the time she was twelve years old, but to please her parents she took on a boyfriend when she was sixteen years old. The guy was her best friend and she didn't mind hanging out with him. That was the extent of their relationship, though. She had never slept with a man and she didn't know what it felt like to be with a man. She didn't even have any interest in exploring that territory.

I couldn't understand why she didn't like to be poked by a man, but she had a box full of vibrators. It may not have been a dick going inside her, but something was going in there and she was obviously getting off on it. I wondered if Tanya was really a hypocrite in disguise. As intrigued as I was with her description of how soothing a woman's touch made her feel, I could not be swayed from a good dick. I love dicks and nothing can ever change that. Tanya and I decided later on that night to take a short drive down to the University of Massachusetts at Amherst to a party at the Malcolm X house that was held annually by the Black Student association at the school. There are many colleges and universities around the Amherst, Springfield and Holyoke area and they aren't located that far apart.

Before I met Tanya, I was thinking about Darren and how I was going to miss his touch, his kisses and especially his big dick. But Tanya took my attention away from Darren. I knew that she and I would be good friends because we would never have to fight over a man. Tanya had made her position clear and I understood that she was into the licky licky while I was strictly dickly. However, I wasn't sure if I made my position clear to Tanya. Yeah, I knew that I loved dicks, but I was a little curious about what she was telling me about women. Still,

I didn't want Tanya to think that I was tri-sexual. I wasn't willing to try anything sexually just yet. I was still on a dick high that Darren left with me before he went to school.

Chapter 11

We arrived at the party around eleven o'clock and it was jumping. The DJ was playing De La Soul's "Potholes in my lawn" and everyone was getting their groove on. I noticed that all eyes were on Tanya from the time we stepped into the party. I received a few glances myself, but not like Tanya. Little did the guys know that Tanya was looking for the same shit they were looking for, a nice pussy to lick! A couple of brothers walked over to us and asked us if we wanted to dance. The look on their faces and the arrogance to think that they could just come over and ask us to dance without giving us a chance to case the whole joint was comical. We were getting ready to shut them down as hard as we could, but they noticed the change in our demeanor and changed their tune. They wanted to converse with us. I was very cordial to the taller one who reminded me a little bit of Chris because he was also from Brooklyn. Tanya shut down his friend almost immediately. She didn't even bother telling him her name.

After Tanya shut his friend down, the guy that I met whose name was Bobby, followed his friend to the other side and I told him that I would talk to him later because Tanya and I were going to walk around to check the place out. I could tell that Bobby was excited about meeting me because he was skipping like a little girl back to his friend. I went to the party for one thing and one thing only, to party. I paid three dollars for the admission and no one was gonna keep me from partying. I started to notice this miserable look on Tanya's face after we walked around the room. I'm not sure if it was because she didn't see any other lesbians at the party or if she didn't see anyone who fit her type, but I was not going to let a party pooper ruin it for me.

After about a half hour of standing around in the room and watching everyone dance to EPMD's hit "Gold digger", Bobby finally mustered enough courage and balls to come back and ask me to dance. I danced with him for half the night to some of the hottest Hip Hop music, but it wasn't until the DJ switched the music to reggae that I started getting into Bobby. The DJ was playing Shabba Rank's "Mr. Lover man". Bobby held on to my waist and started grinding on me until his dick got hard to the point where I could feel it on my back. I could tell he was packing a good ten inches and his dick was thick. From the movement of his pelvis to the reggae beat, I could tell that he knew how to put it down in the bedroom as well. I made the decision that Bobby was going to be my dick supply that night. I ended up spending the whole night dancing with Bobby. Before I knew it, he was grabbing my ass and feeling me up with pleasure. At the end of the night, I asked him if he wanted to come back to my school with me. Of course, he couldn't turn down a girl who was wearing the shortest poom poom shorts that she could find in her closet.

Just like that, I had started to forget about Darren. My sexual appetite was immediate and I needed to satisfy my hunger for dick. Tanya was mad when we were driving back to Mount Holyoke. She wasn't as lucky as me that night. I parked the car and I ran up to my room with Bobby in tow and to my surprise, my roommate still had not reported to the school. I had the liberty to fuck Bobby all over the room any way that I wanted to. Bobby was cute, but he wasn't anything to brag about. I was more impressed with his moves than his looks. We got totally naked and Bobby didn't disappoint. He was packing a ten-inch dick that was just as thick as Darren's. Ten inches was comfortable to me as long as he knew how to work it.

Bobby must've attended the same pussy eating school as Darren because he had me sitting on top of my desk with my legs wrapped around the back of his neck as he went to work on my pussy like a love doctor. He ate me like he was on death row and I was his last meal request before his execution. My legs started shaking as he stuck his long tongue in and out of my pussy. I leaned my body back against the wall as Bobby knelt on the floor and continued to eat me until I came all over his mouth. We switched positions; Bobby sat on my desk while I sat in the chair to suck every inch of his ten-inch dick very slowly. I took the head of his dick in my mouth and I applied enough suction to drive him nuts. Bobby couldn't handle my skills and he came within thirty seconds after I had my tongue wrapped around his dick. I thought I was once again in the company of a preemie.

He apologized to me and told me that he couldn't control it, and promised that his second nut would last all night. He wasn't lying about that. Bobby almost tore my pussy to pieces as he banged me around the room every which possible way. He had me bend over the chair as he penetrated me from the back and unloading his extraordinary waist movements on me the same he was moving to that reggae music on the dance floor. His rhythm was causing me to explode almost every fifteen minutes. At one point, he had me upside down on the chair with my legs wrapped around the back of his neck while he ate my pussy. It was easy for him to eat me to submission because my arms supported my whole weight while he simply had to hold on to my thighs and eat my pussy until he satisfied his hunger. He was one pussy eating king. Even Darren didn't eat me as well as Bobby. He and I fell asleep around five o'clock in the morning after we exhausted all our energy fucking each other around the room.

Chapter 12

I woke up the next morning feeling completely out of it and I had my first class scheduled for ten o'clock. I had to get up, jump in the shower then drive Bobby back to his campus at U-Mass. and I only had one hour to do all of that. I woke Bobby up and told him that we had to get a move on because I didn't want to miss my first day of class. He told me not to worry about it because most of the students usually didn't show up for their first day of class, anyway. Bobby was a sophomore at U-Mass. majoring in computer engineering. He had one year of college experience, which was more than I had and he was studying a field that I never understood because it was too hard for me to grasp. I took his comments as perhaps, something that he knew as fact, but I still didn't want to miss my class.

I gave him some Listerine to get rid of his tart morning breath when I came out of the shower. I threw on my Gap sweat suit and I was out the door. I made it to U-Mass. in no time and I told Bobby that I would call him later after I dropped him off. That mother fucker wore my ass out. It was a good thing that my mother bought me a bunch of sweat suits before I left for school, because I would not have had enough time to iron my clothes and make it to class on time. I stumbled into class just before the professor closed the door. It was refreshing to be in a room with a group of young adults where ideas and opinions were being shared. My first class was philosophy and we pretty much went over the syllabus and the expectations that the professor had of us as students. He didn't even keep us for the whole period.

It was 10:50AM when I walked out the classroom, it was a nice sunny autumn morning and I was hungry. Bobby had taken every ounce of energy that I had left in me the night before. I went by Tanya's room to see if she wanted to have lunch with me, but she was in class and left me a note on my door asking me to wait for her so we could go to lunch together. I was hungry as hell and this chick was going to be attending class for another fifty more minutes. I went outside and sat on the lawn in the plaza to breathe the fresh air of western Massachusetts.

While I was sitting out on the lawn, my mind started drifting and I found myself thinking about being with another woman. All that shit that Tanya had put in my head, raised my curiosity. I started watching the women who walked by and imagined how they would be in bed with me. There were also a few lesbians who walked by hand in hand and a part of me wondered if they would let me watch them have sex.

While I was having my daydreams about women, I felt someone pulling on my shirt and calling my name. It was Tanya. She had read the note that I left taped to her door telling her that I would be sitting out in the plaza. I got up and we walked to the cafeteria to go eat lunch. Over lunch, I asked Tanya if she was mad that I left the party with Bobby. She told me that she was honestly jealous that she didn't find anyone to bring back to her room to tear up her pussy the way mine got torn up by Bobby. Tanya told me she heard the commotion going on in my room and she masturbated to the sound of my voice. I was blushing a little bit, but it was funny coming from her. That girl was so blunt.

Tanya and I were getting pretty comfortable with each other very quickly. I told her that I had fantasies of watching two women make love and if she would allow me to watch her the next time she had an encounter. She told me that it would be impossible to do because she had a roommate, but if she didn't, she would be open to the idea as long as her partner was okay with it. I laughingly suggested that she should come to my room if my roommate didn't show up. I realized that Tanya was real cool and she was going to be my support system for the next four years. I never had a close girlfriend my whole life because I didn't want anybody labeling me a freak for having a huge sexual appetite. I was tired of being judged by women. Tanya was different, though. She was just as freaky as I was and she had a lot more sexual experience than I did even though we were the same age. She may have been sleeping with women, but she was still sleeping with a lot more women than the few men that I slept with.

Chapter 13

A week had gone by and my roommate still didn't show up, I started to wonder if she was ever going to show at all. I went down to the registrar's office and I found out that my roommate decided to cancel her admission to the school and that basically meant that I was going to have the room all to myself for the whole year. As much as I was preoccupied with sex and having a good time, I was just as occupied with my studies. The last thing I wanted to do was to flunk out of school and have my daddy kick me out of his house, or worse, break his foot up my ass when I got home.

I went to class regularly and I tried my best to maintain at least a 3.5 average during my first semester. I allowed nothing to get in the way of my schoolwork, not even the long and tasteful dick of Kevin from Amherst College. I had met Kevin at a party at Amherst. At first, I thought he was one of those brainiacs who thought he knew everything about the world because he was attending one of the top liberal arts colleges in the country. But it turned out that Kevin was from the Roxbury section of Boston. He had attended Latin Academy high school and was offered a full academic scholarship to Amherst. Everything about him was hood. Kevin would change the world at the snap of a finger if he could. All he talked about was going back to his community to help make it better. He majored in sociology, but his real focus was human services.

Kevin stimulated my mind and body in a different way. He was light skinned and handsome. He wore wire rim glasses that made him look very studious and intellectual. But with Kevin, it wasn't just a look. He was actually intelligent. Every time we engaged in one of those thought provoking conversations of his, my panties would get uncontrollably wet and all I could imagine was me on top of him, dominating him and making him beg for mercy for being too smart. I didn't sleep with Kevin the first time I met him only because he had some kind of rally that he was putting together early the next day on his campus for some Black cause.

Kevin was a civil rights activist in the making and he made sure that every complaint filed by the Black students on campus was investigated. He and I got together a week later when I invited him over to my campus to hang out. I hated the fact that my parents forced me to attend an all women's college. They were trying their hardest to keep me away from boys, but they made the mistake of buying me a car for school. Since Kevin didn't have a car of his own, I offered to pick him up on a Friday afternoon just to go hang out. While we were in the car driving to my dorm, Kevin suggested that we go see a movie. I wasn't really in the mood to see a movie because I wanted to take Kevin to my room to screw the hell out of him and tear his ass up. All I could think about while we were in the car was Kevin tied up to my bed screaming big words out to me while his dick was in my mouth.

I knew that I needed to be more aggressive with him and I had to initiate the first move. Kevin was shocked when I turned to him and told him that I wanted to take him to my room to fuck him. I thought he would back out of going to my dorm, being "Mr. politically correct" and all. He didn't even hesitate to tell me "drive straight to your campus". As I was driving to my dorm, I wanted to get an idea about what I was gonna be working with. I started flirting with Kevin in the car. I ran my right hand up his thigh while I kept the left hand on the wheel. I wanted to get him excited, and he couldn't contain himself. He reached over and started massaging my inner thighs sensually with his hands.

I was turned on by him and I wanted to jump his bones right there and then. Kevin's dick was half erected and I could already feel about five inches of it in my hand. As I continued to stroke Kevin's dick, he started getting harder and harder. By the time he reached full erection, I had a good nine inches of grade A beef in my hand. I didn't want to wait until I got upstairs to my room to start fucking Kevin. I went and parked my car behind an old abandoned building near the school. Kevin reclined his seat way back as I crossed the center consul in my Volkswagen, Jetta to make my way across to him. I leaned my head over and started sucking his dick with voracity. He had a perfect size dick and I savored every inch of it in my mouth.

While I was sucking Kevin's dick, he had a couple of fingers inside my pussy pleasing me sensually to the soulful sound of Anita Baker on the radio. My skirt was halfway up my thigh and I wanted to mount Kevin. He was kissing me and touching me in a very sensual way. I could tell that Kevin was going to be very gentle with me. I had never been with a guy who was so gentle and to tell you the truth, it was refreshing. Kevin kissed me for while as he snuck a few more fingers inside my pussy doubling my pleasure. A few minutes later, Kevin decided to kneel in front of me while I sat in the front passenger seat so he could eat my pussy.

I was so wet my juices started flowing down my thigh and onto the seat. I could see Kevin looking up at me after every stroke of his tongue against the tip of my clit and this guy was enjoying the taste of my pussy. He started telling me how good I tasted and I was turned on even more. We switched positions again as both of us moved to the back seat and pushed the front seat up and had the back of the seat leaning forward towards the dashboard. I reached for Kevin's fully erected nine inch dick as he sat in front of me in the back seat and stuck it in my mouth again like a long lost possession discovered.

After much practice with my dildo and Darren's big long dick, I was able to swallow Kevin's whole dick and he enjoyed being completely in my mouth. After sucking his dick for about ten minutes, I took it out of my mouth and held it up while I teabag his nuts down my warm throat and I could see him shaking a little bit. The convulsions from his body suggested that he was about to explode at any moment, but Kevin had more dick control than I thought. He eased himself into a position where he was humping my mouth like it was a pussy. I sat back and took all of him in.

What Kevin and I did next was something that I didn't even think was possible. He flipped me up side down where my head rested between his legs and my legs on the dashboard near the window. He ate my pussy until I screamed that I was coming multiple times. I almost broke the front window of my car because I kicked so hard when I was coming. Kevin took my juices in his mouth and then reached down to kiss me and made me taste my sweet pussy juice. He got off on it. He told me he wanted me to see how I good I tasted. He was right. I loved the taste of my own pussy juice in my mouth. After we kissed for about two minutes, Kevin had me lean face forward on the back of the bucket seats and used the center consul for support to ram my ass from behind. His dick was so good inside of me, I only felt pleasure. I didn't have to worry about him ripping my cervix to shred because he had the perfect size dick. I especially like his long strokes because he hit my g spot just right. The only other man who ever did it perfectly was Darren.

Kevin and I were exhausted about an hour later. We sat in the car and talked for a little while. I invited Kevin to come to my room to spend the night with me. We went at it again and I came over and over again. Kevin had even more tricks up his sleeves when we got upstairs to my room. For a guy who didn't seem all that rough and tough, he was surprisingly good. I would never look at a nerdy looking guy in a funny way again. Kevin was not a nerd however, but his appearance was very close to one.

Chapter 14

Through the course of the school year, I visited Darren a couple of times at Syracuse and he visited me a couple of times as well. During one visit at my school, Darren was fucking me so well, I started screaming very loudly and I woke up everybody on my floor. The next day, all eyes were on Darren and me as we walked out of my building. The white girls especially wondered if Darren was hung like a horse. They kept staring at his crotch whenever they saw us together.

I also found out that Darren was laying more pipes than a whole plumbing company full of plumbers up at Syracuse. We isolated ourselves in his room during the whole weekend while I was there visiting once. We barely did anything on campus. I didn't even get a chance to check out his campus. But it was fine with me because Darren was laying pipes on me ninety nine percent of the time while I was there. He laid his pipes until my pussy got sore and I couldn't take anymore. Sex with Darren was always special to me. He's the only guy that I think I have ever developed true feelings for. I like the way he always tries to protect me, the way he caresses my body, the way he holds me and the way he loves me. He has never had a problem expressing his feelings for me.

That year, I probably fucked about ten guys at school, but a lot of them aren't even worth mentioning because they couldn't deliver the goods. There was one guy in particular who thought his dick was the bomb diggy. I don't know who lied to him, but he thought he was the best thing walking this earth. Little did he know, he was the worse partner that I had ever been with. For a guy who was so cocky, he had a lot of doubts and questions about himself when we were having sex. He kept asking stupid questions like "Is this pussy mine?" I wanted to ask, are you the one taking this weak ass dick inside you right now? I should've just scream "Hell no! It's not your pussy".

He continued, "Do you love this dick? Is this the biggest dick you ever had?"Who the hell has time to take a quiz while they're fucking? "Save the fucking questions for your professors at school, just tear my mother fucking ass up and shut the fuck up" is really what I wanted to say to him. And I would run into this asshole every where I went and he thought he would get more ass each time. One day I had to come out and straight dis his ass. He kept bothering me while I was at a party, fucking up my game with other potential good dick suppliers. I told him to quit bugging me, but he insisted on telling me that he was gonna tear my pussy to shreds the next time he fucked me. But he had it coming.

I really had to compose myself because there was so much I wanted to tell that mother fucker. "Look, you little dick mother fucker. You can't fuck, you can't eat pussy, you can't move, you don't know what the fuck you're doing and you talk too goddamn much. Get the fuck out my face before I embarrass your ass some more" is all I could say as I went off on him. That whole shit came out of nowhere from me because I was fed up with his ass. Afterwards, I even thought I held my tongue back a little because I could've said so much more. I wasn't sorry that everyone within earshot heard what I said to him. I was pissed because it was bad enough that I gave him the benefit of the doubt by taking him home with me, but he had the nerve to think his dick was good when his shit was trash. I didn't like to waste my time or my pussy on mother fuckers who were all talk. After that episode, he stayed totally clear of me. I'm sure he went back and reevaluated his skills and he probably wondered how many other women were laughing at his clown ass.

Whenever I wanted some good dick, I simply picked up the phone and call Kevin or Bobby. I alternated between the two of them that whole year. I had to cut Kevin off by the end of the school year, though. He was making plans to come to New

York in the summer to visit me and chill with me for a weekend. I felt that he was getting too attached. When I was in New York, I only needed one man and that was Darren. Darren and I had plans to have sex all over Central Park in Manhattan, Jones Beach in Long Island, Prospect Park in Brooklyn and every where in between. We had planned on having a lot of fun that summer.

I felt bad about cutting Kevin off because he wanted to know the reason why we couldn't continue to see each other. He wasn't the type of guy to accept a situation for what it was. He was good dick supply that I needed while I was at school and I probably would have continued to give him ass every year until I graduated from college, but his ass wanted to get all emotional and shit. I couldn't pick any guy over Darren, he was my number one and he always will be.

Bobby on the other hand, was a bad boy who knew exactly what I needed from him. He never even called to ask me to chill with him once. He just made himself available whenever I needed some good dick. Bobby also enjoyed being with me because he thought that I was down for whatever. He never asked questions about any other guys like Kevin did all the time. He knew my pussy was mine to do anything I wanted with it. Kevin used to give me attitude and sometimes he would act like a little bitch if I couldn't see him. I warned him from the beginning that I was nothing to play with and I was not looking for a relationship, but he didn't listen. He allowed my pussy to become his weakness. Bobby was carefree and on the hunt just like I was. He knew how to have fun and control his emotions at the same time. He wasn't fazed by pussy, but he enjoyed a good one. I really liked Bobby too, but I still preferred Darren.

Chapter 15

Tanya and I had a lot of fun during our freshman year in college. Tanya was fucking the women while I took on the men. We slept with at least ten to fifteen partners every year and we fucked almost everyday. Tanya's numbers may have been a little higher than mine. The whole campus was aware of our sexual escapades and we didn't give a damn. Those people didn't pay our tuition. The only time I believed that Tanya didn't have sex was during finals like me.

During finals week, Tanya spent most of her time at the library studying. We didn't go to any parties and our phone was usually off the hook when we were in our rooms studying.

I was not interested in dick during finals. Like I said, I didn't want my dad breaking my neck for flunking out of school. My parents gave me an allowance every week so that I didn't have to work. They wanted me to focus completely on school. They paid for my room and board because I had gotten a four-year academic scholarship from the school. I was living stress free and worry free. My only concentration was school and I made sure I excelled. Tanya's situation, however, was a little different. She didn't have a scholarship and she didn't have wealthy parents to help pay her tuition. She was a first generation college student busting her ass to make the grades. And as a pre-med major, her classes were very hard consisting of a lot of science related subjects like biology and all those other classes that I tried my best to stay away from.

Tanya was very smart and she had a lot of pressure on her. The oldest of five children, she had to set a good example for her brothers and sisters. Tanya was also the pride of her parents. They couldn't stop telling people how great of a daughter she was. Tears would flow down Tanya's face every time she talked about her parents. As much as they claimed they loved and were proud of her, Tanya feared that they would disown her if she revealed her true sexual orientation to them.

Tanya had only decided to be open about her sexuality when she arrived at Mount Holyoke College. She had been living a secret life back home and she was tired of it. At school, she was a liberated woman who lived her life the way she wanted. I sympathized with her, not just as friend, but also as a person. Even during the summer breaks Tanya chose to stay on campus because she dreaded the idea of going back home and living a fake lifestyle. She would always tell her parents that she needed to take a few extra classes and she wouldn't be home for the summer. That went on for the whole duration of her college career.

Chapter 16

While Tanya was worried about telling her parents that she was gay, I was making sure that my parents didn't find out that I was acting like a little slut on campus. It would have been heart broken for my dad to learn that I was sleeping with every Tom, Dick and Harry that I could find with a good tool. It would be something close to homicide for me. I believe that I inherited my freaky ways from my parents, but the difference was that they were monogamous.

They offered to visit me on campus quite often, but I always made up an excuse that I had to study for an exam so that they wouldn't come. The few times they insisted on coming, I spent most of the time with them at their hotel because I didn't want them to hear the rumors circulating about me around the school. To be honest, they weren't really rumors. I had fucked just about as many guys that I was rumored to fuck, but my parents didn't have to know that. I was still their innocent little girl.

Even when my brother would beg me to allow him to come for a visit, I would lie to him and pretended that Tanya was my roommate. My brother, Will, was a trip. Will wanted to come see me because I attended an all women's college and he made sure that I was aware of the fact that he wouldn't need to stay with me. He told me that he was sure to find a few women who would be more than willing to spend a night filled with fun and hot sex with him. My brother and I were close and we talked on the phone almost every day. He had decided to attend Rutgers University in New Jersey so he could play football. He was recruited by many schools, but he chose Rutgers because he wanted to stay close to home.

Will was just as much of a ho as I was in college. When I visited him at Rutgers, he was spending his nights with a different woman almost the whole time I was there. So many women came by his room to see him while I was there I wondered how he ever got any work done at all. My brother managed to maintain a B average the whole time he was in school. Since he was two years older than me, he graduated when I was still a sophomore in college and was drafted in the upcoming draft by an NFL team in the south. I didn't have to worry about him visiting me during my last two years of college because he was too busy and too large to come to my school.

Even though Will and I resemble each other a little, I was still getting dirty looks when I walked with him on his campus. The female vultures couldn't keep their hands off my brother. He used to tell me about how he used to twist these girls out and they could never get enough of his big dick. My brother and I were cool to the point where he didn't mind telling me he had a big dick. I knew he did because I used to watch him and his girlfriend go at it when I was younger. My brother finally managed to make it to my school one weekend however, he ended up spending most of his time at U-Mass. He met some girl there that he just couldn't get enough of. It was a good thing because, my brother would have probably hooked up with one of those chicks on my campus who hated me and they probably would have spilled my business out to him without realizing we were related. Those bitches were always hatin'.

Chapter 17

During our senior year in school, Tanya and I decided to move in together to an off-campus apartment. We wanted the freedom to do whatever we wanted during our last year of school. To be honest, we were growing tired of being under the scrutiny of the other students. It seemed like they were always watching and talking about us. However, their punk asses would never say anything to our faces. Sometimes, Tanya and I would walk by and bump them to get a reaction from them, but none of them ever reacted. We were a little gangster at school.

After Tanya and I moved into our apartment, we sat down and made up the house rules of our own expectations of each other as roommates. We felt that our friendship was strong enough to carry us through, but my mama warned me that many friendships have been destroyed after two people lived together. I wanted to make sure that didn't happen to me and Tanya. We set our rules and guidelines.

Since Tanya enjoyed cooking and she was pretty good at it, we agreed that I would wash the dishes whenever she cooked and we would take turns cleaning the apartment every week. But we still made up a cleaning schedule so there wouldn't be any disagreements. We also sat down and discussed visitors and how late would be too late to be loud. Tanya knew that I was a screamer during sex and she didn't mind it because she could masturbate to my screams. She was also a screamer, but she wasn't as loud as me. After making sure that we covered every detail regarding our living arrangements, Tanya and I were ready for the final year of our college career. This would be the year that determined our future and we wanted to go out with a bang.

I had planned on fucking everywhere in the apartment except Tanya's room. I was even willing to experiment a little during my last year in school. Since my workload was light because I had taken most of the difficult classes in my major during my junior year, I wanted to dedicate the rest of my time to having fun. There were quite a few guys who wanted to get with me, but I wanted to be very particular with my sex partners during my last year. I didn't like men that talk a lot and I stayed away from psychos and controlling men. I was not going to let any man dictate to me what I could or could not do with my pussy.

Chapter 18

Believe it or not, Tanya and I sat down in our living room and wrote down the names of a few guys and girls that we wanted to sleep with before the school year was over. At the top of my list, was this basketball player from U-Mass. who was rumored to have a dick long enough to choke a mule. I had seen him around campus, but I never paid him any mind because Bobby was the best dick supply that I ever got out of U-Mass. I tried fucking a few other dudes there, but they were no match for Bobby.

A part of me missed him when he graduated the year before me. Bobby was a legend among college men. If I could give a trophy for excellence, Bobby would receive it for the best pussy pounder on campus. That man used to pound my pussy just like I like it. Now, I needed to look for a replacement for Bobby because I just couldn't go without any dick. The replacement I wanted would be none other than that famous basketball player with the big dick that I had been hearing so much about. I didn't even know his name yet, but I knew who he was.

My list was not really that long and extensive. There were a couple of handsome guys that I thought could rock my world at U-Mass. and the neighboring Springfield College and American International College, but I wasn't too eager to find out how good they were. If they stepped to me, I had decided that I would let them have a taste.

I always wanted keep one booty call that I knew would satisfy me for certain when I needed it. I had two during my freshman year, but Kevin and I fell out after the first year. Bobby lasted three whole years with me and he never once mentioned having any strong feelings for me. Maybe my attitude and body language indicated to him that I wasn't trying to get all emotionally wrapped up in him. He kept his distance and supplied me with good dick every time I needed it and that was fine with me.

The infamous guy on my target list that all the women on the University of Massassachuesetts campus were talking about was going to be my ultimate prize that year. I had heard so much about this guy, I wanted to find out if the rumors were true. I never asked anybody to confirm anything that I had heard about him because I didn't want anybody to know my personal business. It was the beginning of the year and I needed to secure my booty call for the year and I needed to do it with class and tact because I was a senior.

I was trying to conjure up a plan to get to my new booty call and the best place to catch him was going to be at the party at the Malcolm X house that was held annually. The only problem was that every single bitch on that campus would be jocking him and I would have to compete with them. I did not like to compete with any woman over a man. I knew that my pussy was good enough and my blowjob skills were out of this world. A woman fighting over dick was petty to me because there were always enough guys willing to make their dicks available as long as there were some legs opened. The only difference was that, there was a lack of good dick.

Tanya's list was outrageous, that bitch had at least twenty names on her list and she promised to fuck every single person on that list. There were a few more potential guys that I wanted to fuck as well, but I didn't make any promises to myself. I was gonna play everything by ear. I was used to getting what I wanted and most of the guys that I had been with told me that I was irresistible. It could've been my pussy forcing them to say the right shit while they were inside of me, but it didn't matter much to me. I was always confident with my game and I knew that I had enough practice to know that my pussy was the bomb!

Tanya was quite the expert in the bedroom herself. There wasn't a woman that she had gotten with who didn't scream for mercy. Tanya even admitted to me that she could eat a pussy until her mouth was incapacitated. Now, that was a pussy eating chick. Occasionally, my own pussy got wet when Tanya demonstrated, with the movement of her lizard tongue, how she would eat a woman until she came. I was also surprised at the many lesbian and bisexual women we found on the different college campuses that we visited. I always imagined lesbians as big butchy women wearing construction boots and plaid shirts. Tanya put to rest all those stereotypes very quickly. She was bringing women home as feminine and classy as Nicole Kidman. Most of the women Tanya slept with were as gorgeous as she was. However, she did appear to be the domineering person in her relationships and brief encounters.

Chapter 19

The day of the party finally came and Tanya and I were planning to score with our target folks no matter what it took. One of the first things I did that day while I was lounging in my room was search through my closet and lay out all my revealing clothing. I wanted to wear an "attention getter" that night because I didn't want to miss my target. This was something new that I had never done, but because it was my last year of school, I didn't give a damn. Tanya expected a couple of people on her list to be at that party as well. When I told her my plans to wear something as outrageously hoochie as possible, Tanya was onboard with me. We had quite a few hoochie outfits to choose from and we had hoped to make up our minds by the time we got back from dinner. Tanya and I ate at the cafeteria sometimes, when we were too lazy to make anything to eat at home. She rarely ate anything I cooked, anyway. Even I didn't like the stuff that I cooked, so I didn't blame Tanya for not eating my cooking.

Ten O'clock had arrived and it was time to get ready for the party. Tanya and I must've taken the longest showers that evening. We made sure our coochies were squeaky clean. By the time we left the house to go o the party, it was quarter past eleven. Of course, we had taken with us some brew to get nice before we actually went into the party. We were feeling quite nice after guzzling down a couple of vodka nips mixed with coke. It was time for us to head to the Malcolm X house and be seen.

When we walked in, all eyes were on us. I specifically wore these poom poom shorts that barely covered my ass with knee high boots and a tube top that revealed my firm and toned stomach and held my double D breasts up. I was in all black and Tanya wore a red mini skirt and a red halter top with black boots. We looked like two hoochie mamas who came to the party to steal everybody's man and woman. I would round up the men and Tanya would capture the women.

I could see the hate on the women's eyes because they couldn't believe that we were that bold with our outfits. If that mother fucker with the big dick didn't notice me that night, I didn't need to fuck him period, I thought. We got to the party a little late because we wanted to make a grand entrance and we were going to dance only with the people we wanted to fuck. This was a special night and we weren't going to waste our time.

About ten minutes after we stood there watching everybody, I noticed "Mr. Well Hung" staring at me and smiling. He wasn't as tall as I imagined, but he was at least six feet two inches tall and weighed about two hundred and twenty pounds. I smiled back at him and then I turned to Tanya to tell her that he caught my bait. By then, Tanya was making some eye contacts of her own. One of the girls whose legs she couldn't wait to get her tongue between, had a big Kool-Aid smile on her face directed at Tanya. We were both about to get our mack on. We were standing there calling our admirers all kinds of name in the book. I said to Tanya "I hope he brings his punk ass over here soon because I don't have much patience for shy people'. Tanya's game was a little different than mine she was always the aggressor. That bitch walked right over to the other chick and left me standing there by my goddamn self. I guess it was a good thing because Mr. Daddy Long Strokes made his way towards me in no time.

He introduced himself as Ricky but people called him Rick for short. I playfully referred to him as Pretty Ricky. He smiled and told me "The only pretty person I see here is you". I was surprised he had a little game. Ricky was the senior point guard on the team. It was his fifth year in school because he had red shirted as a freshman. We talked and danced for a little while. He wasn't the best dancer to Hip Hop music. I was hoping that the DJ would play some reggae so I could size up his manhood and bedroom abilities. Around two o'clock in the morning, I told him that I was leaving the party and asked if he wanted to come home with me. Ricky didn't even wait for the offer to completely make its way out of my mouth before he said "sure!" I wanted so much to confirm all the rumors about the size of his dick that I had been hearing about before I took him home with me.

As luck would have it, the DJ started playing reggae just as we stepped outside of the door. It was my chance to get him excited on the dance floor so I could feel his dick rubbing against my ass. I pulled him back into the party and told him that I wanted him to dance with me. He didn't hesitate to honor my request. We got on the dance floor, but Ricky was not as good a dancer as he probably was a ball player. I gave him the benefit of the doubt and thought that maybe he didn't know how to move to reggae. I grabbed his hands and placed them on my hips as I leaned back to do "the bogo" dance. Ricky was rubbing my ass and I could feel the monster unfolding in his pants like The Incredible Hulk after someone made him angry. Ricky confirmed the rumors and my suspicions. He had to be at least a good fourteen inches and that was something that I never had before. Darren possessed the biggest dick that I had ever seen or fucked and I wondered if I was gonna be able to hang with Mr. "Well Hung".

The thought of him tearing my pussy up was excruciating, but if he knew how to work his tool, I wouldn't have to worry, I thought. After the reggae music stopped and I confirmed what I wanted to know, I told Ricky that I was ready to leave. The only thing he said to me was "Let's go!" all excitedly. I was in a rush to get home to get my ass torn up by his big dick. I went over to Tanya and told her that I was leaving with Ricky. She told me to go ahead because she was going to spend the night with her new friend that she had just met. I guess we were both going to get our groove on that night. I was looking forward to fucking the hell out of Ricky all over my apartment.

As I drove to my apartment, Ricky reclined his chair back and pulled his dick out and started playing with himself. He warned me that he had a huge dick and he was nothing to fuck with. I reached over to palm his dick and I made a comment that his dick was only about eight inches. Ricky retorted "You must have a measuring problem because you're looking at fourteen inches of prime beef and I know how to work it too". I admired his confidence, but I still hoped he wasn't all talk like some of the guys that I had been with.

We stopped at the red light and while he was massaging his dick, I leaned over and placed my mouth on the head and that shit almost filled up my whole mouth. He had a mushroom dick. The head was like a big umbrella and the rest of it was thick and long. I knew that I was gonna enjoy sucking it because I could tell he wasn't a preemie. I was already lost in his dick because the person behind me kept beeping after the light had turned green and I didn't even notice. His dick tasted so good, I didn't want to take it out of my mouth.

I drove as fast as I could to get to my apartment. As we walked through the hallway down to my apartment, a few of the female residents in my building noticed the huge bulge in Ricky's pants and most of them couldn't believe it. It almost looked like he stuffed his underwear with a bunch of sox, but I knew the real deal and couldn't wait to be his holy field. I walked in the apartment and Ricky asked me to put on some reggae music because he enjoyed my movements on the dance floor and he wanted a private dance. I went through my CD collection and I found my Shakka Demus and Pliers CD. The tune 'Murder She Wrote" was on cue as I made my way back to the couch to stand in front of Ricky to start dancing. As the music played, I started to slowly caress my body with my hands while moving to the Caribbean rhythm and gazing into Ricky's eyes. He yelled for me to take my tube top off as he pulled his dick out of his pants and started stroking it back and forth with his hand playing with himself. By the time I exposed my double D breasts to him, his fourteen inches stood fully erect and he kept massaging the head with his hand.

I bent over and stuck my ass up in the air near Ricky's face as I continued to grind to the reggae beat. While my ass was sticking up in the air, Ricky pulled my poom poom shorts to the side with one hand and stuck his index finger inside me while he continued to play with his dick using his other hand. I pulled my body back up as I felt the thrust of his finger inside my pussy causing my wetness to run down to the side of my left thigh. Ricky took the finger out of my pussy and stuck it in his mouth tasting my sweet pussy juice. I stood in front of him and lifted my left leg up and placed it over his right shoulder as I continued to wind to the music. Ricky couldn't help himself when the sweet aroma of my pussy hit his face. He deserted his dick as he wrapped one hand around my butt and the other to pull my shorts to the side so he could stick his tongue inside of me. He ate my pussy while one of my legs rested over his shoulder until my other leg couldn't stand it anymore. He wanted to lay me down on the couch to finish the great oral treatment that he had started, but I stopped him.

The boots that I wore turned Ricky on, so he requested that I kept my boots on after he pulled my shorts off me. I stood in my living room totally naked wearing nothing but my knee-high boots. Ricky sat back and admired every curve on my body while he jerked off. He asked me to play with myself and I spread my legs open to rub my clit. I had never been so hot. Watching Ricky masturbate while I played with myself really got me hot. As he gave me instructions to finger myself, I could see his body jerking like he was about to come. He stood up and pulled me towards him and splattered his semen all over my back.

It was my turn now to show him my skills. Ricky never lost his erection after he came. After wiping his semen off my back with a towel, I returned to the living room to find Ricky sitting in my recliner with his legs wide open and his dick reaching for the ceiling. I knelt between his legs and I started licking the head of his dick, which filled up my mouth to capacity. I went up and down and around his dick with my tongue until I satisfied my chocolate hunger. His dick was like a big chocolate candy bar to me. Looking at Ricky's big ass light pole that he called a dick, I knew that I couldn't deep throat it and I didn't even bother trying. I was amused that it was so huge, so I just caressed it with my tongue until my mouth was sore. I could tell that Ricky was enjoying my tongue action because he didn't want me to come up for air as he kept moaning and screaming "suck it. Keep sucking it, don't stop".

After sucking him off until my jaw hurt, he pulled me up on the chair and I tried to straddle him. Only half of his dick was inside me when I started coming all over myself like a running faucet. I couldn't really handle Ricky's big ass dick. He had me stick my ass up in the air and my face on the floor while he slowly stroked me and tore my pussy up like he owned it. His slow winds thrust his dick inside my pussy and he hit all the right spots. Moments later, he would have me lean across the top of the couch on my back balancing me with his dick inside of me. I felt like I was holding on for dear life. Ricky never got rough with me, but his dick was doing some damage. By the time Ricky reached his second orgasm, I was worn out and ready to go to sleep, but he wouldn't let me got to sleep and my pussy kept throbbing for more every time I looked at his long dick.

That night he fucked me every which way until I came over and over again. I wanted to see if I could take all his fourteen inches inside of me, but when he got to about twelve and a half, I had enough. I couldn't take the whole thing, at least in the beginning. Ricky had certifiably become my dick supplier for my senior year. I fucked a lot of other guys that year while I was still fucking with Ricky, but none of them even came close to what he had. Ricky wanted to stroke me hard at times, but he could not get rough with me because his dick was too big. I didn't want to get crippled by him.

Chapter 20

I had a blast during my senior year in college. I slept with most of the guys on my target list and then some. But Ricky was the one guy that I ever met and was afraid of. He had a huge dick and he knew how to use it. Like Bobby, Ricky didn't bother me and he understood our arrangements. There were a couple of guys who tried stalking me, but Ricky was able to get rid of them when he showed up with a couple of his basketball teammates to explain to them the ramifications of messing with one of his close friends. No physical fight ever took place, though. Ricky and his friends' presence alone took care of my problem.

I also had my first lesbian encounter during my senior year. It was with none other than my roommate and best friend, Tanya. Tanya knew that I was always bi-curious and the attraction between her and I was undeniable. I always thought that she was a beautiful woman and I would get wet when she'd start telling me about her sexual encounters with other women. One night after coming home from a lame party where all the men were absolutely corny and horrendous looking, I found myself sucking on Tanya's tits while she caressed my hair. It was the first time I had ever had a nipple in my mouth and to be honest, I found it extremely hot. I sucked on her breasts sensually until she started moaning and her moaning took me to another place. I felt like Tanya was at my mercy and I had the upper hand because I was giving her pleasure.

My domineering feeling continued as I went down to Tanya's navel, licking every inch of her body while she closed her eyes to enjoy the wonderful movement of my tongue all over her body. Tanya grabbed one of my hands and placed it down on her pussy as the sensation from my tongue intensified her need to reach ecstasy. I felt powerful when I saw the look on Tanya's face while I was licking her body. I could see Tanya getting weaker every time I sucked on her nipples. I enjoyed playing with her perky breasts and they were a mouthful. I made my way back down pass her navel down to her crotch just long enough to tease her.

As much as she would have liked for me to go down and eat her pussy, I stopped and went back up and started French kissing her. Tanya's tongue was smooth and her lips were soft. Her kisses were perfect as she reached out for my tits and started caressing them with her hands. Tanya made me feel something that I had never felt before. Yes, I was satisfied with men, but Tanya was doing things to me with her hands that I had never experienced with a man. She rubbed my nipples with her hands and softly press and rubbed on them with the tips of her fingers. My pussy was drenched with my flowing juices and before I knew it, Tanya had me lying on my back and licking my breasts until I came. In the past, I had never come while someone was just sucking my tities. By the time Tanya reached my navel and was headed for my clit, I was trembling and didn't know what to expect. She was an expert with her tongue as well and was about to wear my ass out with it.

She had her hand in my crotch rubbing my clit while she kissed around my navel in a circular motion. My pussy was hot and wet and the only thing I could do was close my eyes and allow her to take me to seventh heaven. When Tanya finally made her way down to my clit, she started doing tricks with her tongue that I could not describe. She sucked on my erected clit like it was a miniature dick while finger fucking me with her index and middle finger. I was screaming like I never screamed before and before I knew it I was begging Tanya to stop because I was about to reach the most explosive orgasm that I had ever reached. Afterwards, the only thing Tanya could say to me was "I knew you'd like it if you tried it". Tanya knew that she had turned me out a little and I couldn't wait to enjoy her tongue action during the last few days of school.

Tanya wasn't the only action that I got before I graduated from college. Ricky continued to come by to smash my ass whenever I needed some good dick. I didn't want Tanya to strap on her dildo to fuck me when I had good dick at my disposal. I noticed that she would get jealous whenever Ricky came over. I had to make it clear to her that I was not a lesbian and nor did I plan on becoming a lesbian because I still loved a good dick inside of me. Tanya may have been good with the tongue, but I needed a man to be satisfied completely. I never let Ricky in on my secret with Tanya. He had a hard time figuring out why she always had an attitude when he was around.

My college experience is something that I will never forget. I did things that sometimes were unimaginable, I had fun, I experimented with different people and different toys, I partied my ass off, but most of all, I enjoyed myself. One of my only regrets that I have is that I didn't get to spend as much time with Darren as I wanted to. While he was busy fucking his whole campus at Syracuse, I occupied my time with the guys at U-Mass, Amherst College, Springfield College and even a few scrubs from American International College. Everyone was serving me from everywhere and I loved it! I walked away unscathed because there was never any emotions attached to any of the men that I slept with in college. Darren will always be the one and only guy that I love and I couldn't wait to finish school to be near him again.

The other regret that I had was my fall out with Tanya. She had started to become quite demanding of my time the last few weeks of school after we slept together. I never saw it coming and if I knew, I would've never allowed myself to get caught up in Tanya's lesbian world. I didn't regret the experience of being with a woman, but I wanted my friendship with Tanya to last forever.

Chapter 21

As a psychology major, I didn't really know what I wanted to do after I graduated from college. One of the things that I considered was a PhD. in psychology and the other was to pursue a doctorate in sociology. I couldn't make up my mind on which one would be more satisfying to me, but I knew that I wanted to help people in the future. I had more than enough time to think about my future plans. Meanwhile, I wanted to spend as much time as possible with Darren while we were in transition with our futures. Darren's plans were much more solid than mine. Since he studied accounting as an undergrad, he knew he wasn't going to have any problem finding a job and his future plans included taking the CPA exam to become a Certified Public Accountant.

Darren however, decided to take a month off before he entered the workforce for the rest of his life. He had also been promised a full-time job at the accounting firm where he held an internship for the last three years. I was glad that he decid-ed to take a month off because I was hungry and thirsty for his loving. I hadn't spent much time with him since we went away to school. Just watching Darren walk got my panties so wet, one would think that there was a flowing stream down my pants. I missed the touch of his hands, his beautiful smile, his rippled body, his passionate gaze and most of all, his big dick. Darren knew that I couldn't be around him without get-ting some from him. I wanted to make sure that I spent a lot of time with Darren before he started working.

Since my family had become very familiar with Darren over the years, it was not unusual for him to spend time with me at my house. My brother was no longer living at home and my parents were more than happy to welcome me back after I graduated. My dad had offered me a front-office job, but I told him that I wanted to get things done on my own. Darren and I spent a lot of time in the basement at my house watching television and fucking all over the couch. There was one particular time when my mother came downstairs to do the laundry and Darren and I had been getting busy. She almost caught me riding Darren's big dick as she made her way down the stairs. I heard the footsteps, but I was not paying attention. It wasn't until my mother asked if I was downstairs that I noticed her feet making their way down to the basement before she could actually come down low enough to see anything. I was sitting on Darren and he was banging away without realizing that my mother had just spoken to me.

Before my mother could reach the last staircase that would bring her head low enough to see us in the back room, I jumped off of Darren's dick and I pulled my skirt down to act like the proper young lady that she had known me to be. Unfortunately, Darren was not as quick as I was. He didn't pull his pants back up quick enough, but thank goodness he was wearing a long t-shirt. His pants were only pulled up to his thighs with his t-shirt hanging down below his knees.

My mother must've thought that Darren was wearing his pants below his ass like the rest of the young men across the country on every American city street, because she didn't say anything. I think he also lost his erection at the sight of my mother, which I was grateful for. There was no way that he could've hidden that big thing under his shirt without my mother noticing. We came that close to being busted by my mother and wouldn't you know it, we picked up again right after she went upstairs. That was one of the things that I liked about Darren. He was willing to take risk and sex with him was more enjoyable as a result.

Chapter 22

That summer Darren and I also decided to go to Barbados for a week for a getaway. My parents paid for my trip as a graduation gift. Darren's parents were so proud of him; they paid for his trip and even offered to get him a brand new car when he got back. We went down to Barbados the second week in June. We landed at the airport at exactly 12:00PM on a Friday afternoon. The hot Caribbean air of Barbados smacked us right in the face as we made our way down the attached escalator on the plane. Walking down the runway to get to customs seemed like eternity and when we finally made it there, the line was longer than a supermarket line during a snow blizzard warning in New York City. However, the line moved pretty quickly and we were out of there in no time. We caught a cab to St. Lawrence Gap where we were staying, which was a modest hotel located across from a beautiful beach. Darren and I didn't know much about Barbados, so we were excited about the whole experience.

One of the things we noticed quickly about Barbados was that the people there were very friendly. The cab driver was very helpful as he told us where to go to hang out and some of the best restaurants in Bridgetown, the capital. The people there were more than willing to give us advice on where to go when we asked. After checking in, the receptionist at the front desk of the hotel was able to direct us to a rental car place located a few blocks down from the hotel. We rented a car that was so small that Darren had to push his seat way back to get in the car to drive. Although people in Barbados drove on the left side of the road as they do in England, Darren figured he could navigate through the traffic by following the cars in front of him. We also found out very quickly that driving in Barbados was challenging. It seemed like everyone was always in a hurry to get somewhere while we were trying to take our time to enjoy the island.

On the first day, we didn't drive around too much because we were jet lagged from the flight. We lounged by the beach for most of the day until it was time for us to go to dinner. But first, Darren and I had to test the beautiful waters of Barbados. We got in the water at the beach where it was up to our neck and no one even knew that Darren had pulled my bikini bottom to the side so he could insert his twelve inches inside of me while a few hundred people lay nearby on the sand. I wrapped my legs around his body as he slowly stroked me to the rhythm of the waves and caressing my back like we were on our honeymoon.

Every time someone was walking closer to us, Darren would carry me further out with his dick still inside me. The excitement of being voyeuristic prompted my hormones to cause a chemical reaction that forced me to release the tension that was inside me time and time over, at the stroke of Darren's dick inside of me. By the time we decided to leave the water, I was weak and Darren had to carry me on his back. My ass was still trembling as we stepped out of the water to get our towels. People were making comments about how great we looked as a couple. If they knew what we had just done in that water, they all would've packed their bags and call it a day.

Darren and I needed to replenish our energy, so we went back to our room and took a shower. After drying ourselves, we wore the lightest material we brought with us to combat the heat. Darren had on white cotton shorts with a white tank top and white sneakers and I wore a white tennis mini skirt with a pink tube top and a pair of white and pink Nikey sneakers to match. We walked downstairs to the restaurant located at the hotel to eat dinner. Darren wore my favorite cologne for men, Aqua Di Gio by Georgio Armani and I wore his favorite perfume, Forever by Alfred Sung. The scent of the cologne on Darren's body almost caused me to talk him into a quickie before dinner. I wanted to devour him in the room the moment he sprayed that cologne on his body. Instead, I chilled and allowed us to get something to eat.

We had flying fish and rice and beans with fried plantains and coleslaw for dinner and the food couldn't taste any better. Darren drank a "Plus", which is a Bajan energy drink, because he knew that he would need all his energy later to please me by the ocean under the moonlight. I specifically wore a mini skirt because I wanted Darren to make love to me later that evening right on the beach. It seemed like Barbados and its blue waters became an instant aphrodisiac for me and Darren from the moment we landed in the country. There's something about the Caribbean sun that brings the heat out in people and it kept me in the mood most of the time I was there. To Darren's credit, whenever I felt horny, he delivered and I couldn't get enough of him while we were in Barbados.

That night after dinner and a long stroll down St. Lawrence Gap, Darren and I got in the rental car and we drove up to the Animal Flower cave at the north point in St. Lucy where we found a cliff overlooking the ocean. Darren parked the car in the parking lot and we walked up the big rocky cliff to watch the deadly waves hit against the big rocks with full speed. After watching the water for a few minutes, Darren pulled me towards him for a long passionate French kiss. As he was kissing me with the wind blowing through my hair, Darren's hands made their way down to my butt cheeks underneath my skirt and before I knew it, he had me laying on the big rock on the ground with my legs wide open and he was eating me to the sound of the waves.

Darren ate me until he satisfied his hunger for a dessert and I couldn't help myself from pulling his twelve inch dick out of his pants to suck on it right there on top of the rock. Being out in the open made Darren taste so good that night, I didn't want to stop sucking him. Darren made me come a few times when he was eating me and I wanted to return the favor. I sucked his dick and massaged his balls with my hands until he succumbed to my prowess and sent his thick semen down my throat like a tasty vanilla flavored yogurt from a Caribbean farm. I took every drop of him down my throat and that turned Darren to a sexual demon.

He pulled me up towards him and turned me around with my head bending forward facing the water. Darren was not even patient enough to wait for me to pull my underwear off, he pulled them to the side and glided his dick inside of me and started humping me from the back until I felt this tingling sensation that sent me screaming at the top of my lungs that I was coming. It was a scream that he had never heard before because I felt so free and liberated on those rocks. My voice was carried throughout the sea and he just loved it. Darren and I fucked under the moonlight until we got tired and afterwards, he couldn't help telling me how much he loved and missed me. I reciprocated his feelings because I was falling in love with Darren all over again.

That night we drove back to the hotel feeling wonderful. Darren had a big Kool-Aid smile on his face and my own grin was about a mile long from ear to ear. I knew then that Darren was the only man that I could've probably spent the rest of my life with. Not that I was thinking that far ahead, but he was the one. He was sensitive, caring, a beast in bed and had a satisfying dick that I couldn't get enough of.

Though Darren and I didn't spend too much of our time enjoying the nightlife of Barbados, however, we took the time to go see this Soca group called Square One at Tim's in St. James. The lead singer Allison Hines had a body that could make a man squirm and boy could she work it. After watching her that night, Darren came home and tore my pussy apart. I don't know if it was because he had seen Allison wind until he developed a bulge in his pants while I had my back to him in front of the band, but he fucked me like it was a fantasy. We went out on the balcony of the hotel room and Darren had me bent over while holding on to the rails and he put it on me until I begged him to stop because I couldn't take anymore. The sweat pouring down his body while he stroked me made him look like a man possessed. Perhaps, he was thinking about Allison, but I received the benefits of all her hard work on stage.

We also went to see this group called Krossfyah at the After Dark spot in St. Lawrence Gap. Darren and I danced the night away until our waists got tired from winding. Darren was winding on me like he was a native Barbadian. We couldn't deny our African rhythm no matter what the African music was. It could be Hip Hop, R & B, Reggae, Calypso or Soca, our waists always find a way to develop rhythm to the beat. I even noticed a few women staring at Darren's waist as he held on to my hips to wax my backside with his crotch. Just watching the other women salivating over him got me horny enough to leave the party to go back to the beach and allow him to fuck me on some body's canoe that was left tied to an anchor on the water.

We approached the small canoe with caution because we didn't know if the owner was nearby. After sitting on the edge of the boat while Darren held me and caressed my ass for a few minutes without anyone coming to us to say anything, Darren got on the boat and helped pull me up inside the boat. He lay down on his back and asked me to sit up on him to ride him as I kept an eye out for onlookers. Darren may have thought that I was looking out for onlookers, but his dick felt so good inside of me I couldn't keep my eyes open.

The only way I could enjoy riding him was with my eyes closed. It was also the first time that I had ever taken all his twelve inches that deep inside me. In the past, I was too scared to ride Darren, but something about the canoe took away the fear of him tearing my pussy apart. I rode Darren that night until we both reached ecstasy simultaneously. When another couple walked by and noticed the movement of my upper body inside the boat because they couldn't see Darren, they wondered if I was crazy or something. I could hear them whisper to each other and I just kept going because no one was gonna stop me from getting my nut off.

Our vacation in Barbados ended very quickly. It just seemed like time just flew by while Darren and I were having fun. Being in Barbados brought Darren and I closer and I wanted to try my best to keep away from other men while I was home near Darren. My insatiable appetite for sex was something that I had to learn to manage if I were going to be faithful to Darren. Though we never officially told each other that we were going out exclusively with one another, I thought that it was understood.

Chapter 23

The month that Darren had decided to take off to spend time with me before joining the workforce went by pretty quickly. Time always seems to fly when a person is having fun. Darren started his new job at an accounting firm downtown Manhattan while I was still undecided about my next move. I didn't know whether or not I wanted to attend Hunter College to pursue a Doctorate in Sociology or New York University to pursue a PhD. in psychology. Meanwhile, my daddy convinced me to take a job with his construction company because I was getting bored of being home alone all the time. Yeah, I masturbated a lot at home, but I was getting tired of that as well. My position with my father's company was, Office Manager. I pretty much did nothing because my mother was my boss and my father was too busy putting bids in and drawing up plans for the new houses that his company was building all over Long Island.

I wanted to spend my time in Manhattan like Darren did. I wish my father's company was not located in Long Island because there was nothing to do after I got off work everyday. My job was boring and I wasn't sure about what I wanted to do with my life. Darren had a great career that he was excited about while I was in a rut. My dad was trying his best to convince me to be a permanent part of his company, but my heart wasn't quite in it at first.

My brother, Will, had invested some of his NFL money into my father's company and the company grew even more as a result. However, Will wasn't around enough for my dad to groom him for the business. Due to my brother's demanding schedule and gruesome workout regimen for the NFL during the off-season, he couldn't dedicate all his time to the company. The company was more of a safety net for my brother after he retired from football and only then could he dedicate all of his time to it. My brother has always been the type of guy who gave one hundred percent to everything that he was involved with. He assured my dad that the construction company was in his future and when the time comes he would commit himself one hundred and fifty percent.

Since my brother didn't have the time to be groomed for the business, my dad was trying his best to make me his protégée. I really had no interest in construction until my mother showed me the financial records one day. My mouth almost hit the floor when I found out how much money my parents were making. We were multi-millionaires, but they chose to live a normal regular life. As a child, my parents never let me go without and I got almost everything that I ever asked for as long as I behaved in a proper manner, but there was hardly any luxury. The kind of money that I saw raised my interest and I wanted to have a serious talk with my daddy. I had always wanted to live the good life and for the most part my parents provided well for me as a child. However, as a woman, my needs grew and they were very different than when I was a little girl. I could afford to live the high life with the kind of money daddy's company was making.

Although my mother seemed like she was dependent on my father when I was growing up, I never wanted to be like that with a man. My dad happened to be a good man for her and they lived a prosperous life together. I was not naïve to believe that all men would be like my daddy. I also learned that summer that my parents had not given up sex yet either. With the introduction of Viagra, my dad was banging my mother just as much as he did when I was a child. I would come home in the middle of the night and I would hear my mother screaming and telling my dad "give it to me, big daddy. This is your pussy. Take it!" I knew that the apple didn't fall far from the tree, but my mother was a freak. She was quite a few years younger than my dad, and she had a lot of energy. Whenever I think about a long-term relationship, I always hoped to have with Darren the same kind of relationship that my parents have. My mother always supported my father in everything that he did and I wanted to be just as supportive to my future husband.

Chapter 24

After spending a few months learning the ropes at my father's company, I decided to forgo graduate school and dedicated my time to learning the family business. My daddy was very excited and my decision brought us closer than ever. My mother was initially my mentor, but after I figured out her duties a couple of months later, it was time to move on to something else. I have always been a quick learner and when I get excited about something new in my life, I usually pursue it full-force. My parents were impressed with my dedication to the job and I was more than pleased with the high salary that they paid me. There was no other company in corporate America that would pay me as much as my father paid. And I didn't feel a bit guilty about it because my parents had worked hard to establish the business for their children. I wish more Black people would plan more for their kids the way my parents did for me and my brother.

When I was in college, I had friends whose parents never did anything to help them get ahead in life. Sometimes, some of them even had to send their work-study money back home to help the family. I could never understand why some poor people would have five or more children when they can't even provide for one child. There's an old saying "Poor people have kids, so the kids can take care of them while rich people have kids so they can take care of their kids". I found that saying to be true amongst many people that I met and especially the athletes' families. Most of the athletes that I befriended while I was in college had the burden of taking care of their whole family riding on their basketball or football skills. These guys were so stressed about succeeding on the court or on the field that they sometimes neglected their studies so they could excel in sports.

It seems like poor people and middleclass/rich people think differently in terms of family. It's not unusual for a parent who turned his or her back on a child when they were a baby to return only after the child has become successful and expect that child to take care of them. They always used the same old excuse "they gave birth to that child". They want the credit for giving birth, but they don't want to own up to the abandonment of that child. Not to say that rich people don't do that as well, but it's more prevalent with the poorer families where a parent usually come back years later looking to be taken care of.

We can blame the men for turning their backs on their children, but women need to also take on the responsibility of protecting themselves before they lie down with a man who's not suitable to be a dad, especially if that woman has two or three babies by two or three different men already. Nobody's perfect in this world, but there are steps that we can take as people to improve the situations for ourselves and our children. Having four or five baby daddies is not that funny and it never should have been to begin with. I'm just glad that my parents and grandparents were able to break the cycle and now my brother and I don't have to deal with that because we didn't experience it. I hope to have a family of my own one day and I plan on continuing the successful legacy of the family business that my parents have established so that my children and my brother's children will have a better start in the future.

I have even heard stories where the parents died and left the children with their debts. Some people still believe that their debts go away after they've passed. If that were the case, the wife of Sammy Davis jr. wouldn't have been left penniless by her husband after his death. What I find even more appalling are those parents who used their children's names to obtain utility services because they've messed up their own credit. How can a person do that to their own five or six year old child? How are those children supposed to get ahead in life when they're starting life in a hole? I feel that some things are our own responsibilities as individuals and we can't blame society for them.

I really enjoyed working with my dad and I found out very quickly that I liked this line of work. He had me in charge of a few projects of my own in no time and I enjoyed the fact that he entrusted me with the responsibility to help build the company. I found out how hard my dad had to work to get his company off the ground in the beginning, and he explained to me that he never wanted his children to work that hard and that was why he did it. I found out a lot about my daddy after college. I spent so much time with my mom as a child, I knew her like an open book. But my mom would become my best friend as a woman. She started giving me advice about men when she and I would ride to work together. She gave me tips on how to make a relationship work and that it was not dirty to enjoy sex because without sex there would not be a population of any kind on earth.

My mother had no idea that I already knew that she was a freak. I was hoping that she would never find out that I was three times as freaky as she was. I respected my mother because she's only had one partner her whole life, which was my dad. I wondered what she would have done if she knew that I was fucking every Tom, Dick and Harry who possessed a big dick and good sexual skills back in college. Would my mother think that her daughter was a ho? The only guy she ever met was Darren and she thought he was the only man that I had ever been with. And that was a secret that I was willing to keep from her for as long as I could.

My mother did not need to know about my sexual exploits. If she did, the first thing she would've done was run to my father to tell him how much of a ho his daughter really was. I never thought of myself as a ho, but my parents were old school and I didn't want to disappoint them. I could live with the fact that I have an insatiable appetite for sex and that's just what it is. I figure when it's time for me to stop sleeping with more than one guy, I would do it at will. I just wasn't willing to do it yet.

Chapter 25

While I was busy learning the family business, my brother was breaking the backs of running backs in the NFL. He was a decent football player, but not the greatest. Every coach wanted him on their team because of his work ethics and leadership skills. He was also one of the most eligible bachelors in the league. We enjoyed going to his games whenever his team played the Giants or the Jets. My parents never missed any of his games and naturally I had to be there to show support.

To be honest, I never enjoyed watching that brutal sport. I always feared that my brother would one day end up paralyzed on the field because of a play gone bad. As invincible as he thought he was, I worried about him from pre-season until after the playoffs or the Super bowl if his team ever made it that far. My brother and I were very close and there's nothing in the world that I wouldn't do for him or he wouldn't for me, and I know this.

As a football player, I knew that there were plenty of women who appeased him and probably made him feel like a god most of the time. But my parents always made sure that he stayed grounded by telling him that everything that he worked so hard for all his life could be taken away from him at the snap of a finger. They told him that all it would take to lose everything that he abused his body for every Sunday was to sleep with the wrong woman. My brother was never a dumb jock, but my parents made sure that he never let his guard down around women and people in general.

Humility is the key to success and my parents drilled that into his head. They always told him that a simple stroll could've kept Mike Tyson from going to jail for rape. Had he walked that girl back to her dorm, she probably would've been satisfied to be seen with a well-known athlete by the rest of the girls where she was staying. But he was cocky and she made him pay. I think the world knows that Ms. Thang wasn't really raped. It was all about the Benjamins and the white prosecutors are always eager to put a wealthy athlete behind bars to get their names in the paper and their law careers off the ground.

My dad knew that sleeping with different women as a professional athlete was almost inevitable and my brother was no saint. My parents knew that he was a horny bastard since he was a little boy, they just never said anything. I overheard my father talking to my mother about catching my brother masturbating when he was just thirteen years old. Apparently, my brother forgot to lock the door behind him in the bathroom and my daddy's bad habit of not knocking first, allowed him to see something that placed my brother in a compromising position. My brother must've gone to my dad's room and dug into one of his drawers to find a copy of Hustler magazine. He took it in the bathroom with a bottle of lotion and started going to work. According to my dad, Will was so embarrassed he avoided eye contact with my father for a week.

Being the cool father that my daddy was, he had a talk with Will and he told him that it was natural for a boy his age who had just reached puberty to masturbate. My father however, warned him that he should always make sure that the door is locked behind him. As far as the porno magazine, my father never asked for it back. I guess that was his gift to my brother to help him ease the sexual tension. My brother would probably die if he knew that I knew that daddy caught him masturbating in the bathroom.

Chapter 26

Over the years, my brother has also spoiled me with lavish gifts that only a loving brother could buy for his sister. In a way, I felt that my brother wanted to make sure that I wasn't impressed by any guy's bling bling or money. He bought me almost everything I wanted after he signed his big contract and got me used to the finer things. My brother even bought me a convertible Volvo. I was never a materialistic person when I was younger, but as I got older I met a few friends who wanted to introduce me to the trends. Most of the time, they couldn't even afford those trends themselves.

I met this girl in college that I considered more of an acquaintance than a friend. She was all about the latest fashion and jewelry, but her family lived in the projects back home. I really couldn't grasp her reality because she had placed more emphasis on fashion and accessories than she did her education. She ended up pregnant at the end of our freshman year in college by some drug dealer from Springfield, Massachusetts. The girl had potential, but her priorities were all screwed.

I had met those types of guys when I was in college as well, but I could never see past their drug dealing image. I was never impressed with street guys who thought that the destruction of their own community was something to capitalize on. The funny thing about these guys is that they seldom go out of their neighborhoods to sell their drugs. All their customers and victims most of the time end up being people that they grew up with and sometimes even their own family members.

A smart drug dealer is an oxymoron to me. How can someone call himself smart when they know the fate of most drug dealers and still choose to go that route? Most of them suffer the same fate ninety nine percent of the time, dead, in jail or on crack. I'd be damned if I jeopardized my life for some drug dealer. I couldn't last more than a week in jail much less a lifetime. I just love dicks too much to be locked in some prison with a bunch of women because of a crime that some drug dealing boyfriend of mine committed. I don't even want to talk about the possibility of getting shot for being with him. To me, drug dealers just aren't worth the trouble, but more power to the women who think these guys are the best things walking this planet. They can have all of them.

Of course, I do not expect all women to be as fortunate as I am in life, but I require good common sense from them. I've never had too many female friends because I never wanted to get into verbal or physical confrontations over some guy that I could give a shit about. Guys to me were just tools that I used to satisfy my needs. They were not worth fighting over and I never wanted the drama. I guess that's why Darren is the only man that I ever cared about. He had never brought any drama to me until that day when I saw him kissing another woman while I was at this after-work spot in Manhattan.

Chapter 27

Darren had been telling me about this after-work spot called Cheetah's, for professionals that he used to go to with his co-workers after work on Thursdays. Every Thursday he wouldn't get home until one in the morning because he had to hang out at this so called hot-spot. He talked about it so openly, I figured everything that he did there was innocent. That was until I decided to surprise him there on a Thursday. I went to the hairdresser the weekend before to make sure that a sister's hair would be hooked up! On the eve of that Thursday, I had my hair wrapped tight that night before I went to bed to make sure that I look good for Darren and his friends. I had told my dad that I was going to leave work early that day so I could make it to Manhattan by six o'clock, the time that Darren had told me that he usually got there. I left work as planned by four o'clock that afternoon and I hopped in my convertible Volvo C90 to head to Manhattan to Darren's favorite hangout spot at Cheetah's.

While driving on the way there, I felt good. Since it was the fall season, I wore my favorite cream colored wool slacks, my cream colored turtleneck cashmere sweater, my light brown stiletto boots and a light brown designer bag to match. My make-up was flawless and I wore Darren's favorite sweet smelling perfume. I wanted to make an impression on his friends and co-workers. I pulled up at the valet and I handed my keys over to the guy and he handed me a ticket to retrieve my car at the end of the night. I strutted into the club and I could see that my path into the club was parted like Moses parted the red sea. There were men on both sides staring with their mouths open. I paid them no mind at all as I made my way to the bar to order an apple martini. I stood by the bar waiting and looking around for my "Mr. Wonderful" to appear.

After guzzling down a couple of martinis and Darren no where in sight, I decided to walk around the club to see what the big fuss was about.

There were a lot of professional Wall Street types in the club drinking some of the most expensive champagne and throwing around their six-figure salaries to impress some of the floozies who were in the club. Some of them would scream out their salaries a little louder as I made my way by them. I guess they were trying to kill two birds with one stone. They figured if the woman they were talking to weren't impressed enough with their conversation and money, they could always approach the next woman who overheard the big figures. Most men are like boys no matter how old they get. Little boys would go around the neighborhood bragging and showing off their new bikes and clothes, while men brag about their cars and salaries. Sometimes, they are so pathetic.

As I made my way to the back of the club, I noticed a little VIP area where many people were seated. I was trying to catch a glimpse of some of the people in that section when I came across the back of someone's head that looked all too familiar even with somebody else's hand caressing it. I could spot that shiny bald head among millions of bald heads. I knew it was none other than Darren. He had his tongue down this woman's throat while she caressed the back of his head with her eyes closed. I stood there and watched him for a few minutes then I went around making sure I took a good look at his face. After confirming that it was Darren, I made a mental note of his sky blue striped shirt, his solid sky blue tie and his blue blazer hanging over the back of his chair. There was no way he was getting out of this one, but like I said, I was never one to make a scene over a man, not in public, not in private, never!

Even though I was fuming inside, I casually walked away from the back of the club and made my way back to the bar. I wasn't just mad because I felt that Darren was cheating on me, I was mad because the white woman he was kissing was not that attractive and she didn't have to stand up for me to see that she was skeezer. Sure her cup size was a triple D, but only a skeezer would do what she was doing. I didn't want to get mad at Darren; I wanted to get even.

While making my way back to the bar to get another drink, this Italian hunk of a man grabbed my hand and asked if he could have a word with me. Without any hesitation, I said "sure". He asked what I was drinking and I told him apple martinis. He told me his name was Vincent but people called him Vinny and I told him my name was Tina. He and I stood by the bar for a couple of hours and we talked about everything while we sipped our drinks. I noticed that he was not as cocky as the other snobs who were at the club. This guy reminded me of a sexy Johnny Depp with the confidence and suave of Al Pacino. He was good looking, tall and while glancing at his crotch I could tell that he was packing some beef too. I have a bad habit of staring at men's crotches.

I was at the bar until 9:00 PM talking to Vinny and I saw no sign of Darren. He must've been in the back still schmoozing with that skeezer. It was getting a little late and I had to drive down the Midtown tunnel to the Long Island Express Way to get home. I told Vinny that I had a long drive back to Long Island and that I was leaving. Vinny told me that he also lived in Long Island, but he had parked his car at the station and took the Long Island Railroad in to work. He asked if I didn't mind giving him a ride to his car in Long Island, which wasn't too far from where I lived and I said "sure". Vinny had a trusting enough face and to be honest, I didn't mind the company on that long ass ride back home.

Vinny and I went outside and I gave the valet guy the ticket to retrieve my car. We waited for five minutes until the guy came back with my car. I went to pull a ten dollar bill out of my purse to tip the guy, but Vinny beat me to it. He nonchalantly handed the guy a note that looked more like a twenty dollar bill when he shook the guy's hand and told me not to worry about it. He was gaining brownie points with me already. It was a little chilly outside, so I asked Vinny if he minded if I pulled the convertible top up on my car and he said "no". After securing the top, I took off down the street and headed down the Midtown tunnel. I couldn't help but notice how sexy Vinny's dark hair and olive Italian skin looked. He looked like he wore a permanent tan and I could see his muscle bulging through his shirt after he took his jacket off before he got in the car. I had never been with a white man and I never even thought about one until Vinny. Darren made a big mistake that night kissing that bitch and I wanted to pay him back; double.

While driving in the tunnel, the conversation between Vinny and I took a sexual turn. We started talking about some of the wildest places that we ever had sex. Vinny had quite the imagination and when he told me that he was living in a suite on the top floor of this high-rise in Long Island with access to the roof top, he had my attention. I never had sex with anyone on a rooftop before and I could already imagine Vinny's sexy ass fucking me from the back while I hold on to the rail for dear life during an orgasm. My imagination started running wild again and Vinny was reinforcing it with all the things that he was telling me that he would do to me. My pussy was dripping wet watching Vinny's lips uttering words and phrases like "I would lean you against the chimney with your legs spread open while I licked you to ecstasy".

By the time I reached the LIE, Vinny had unzipped my pants and had his finger inside my pussy and I was rubbing his dick with my free hand. For a white guy, I was surprised that he was packing so much meat. His dick had to be at least eight inches long and very thick. I couldn't wait to get my mouth on it. He kept pulling his finger out of my pussy and kept putting it in his mouth to taste my pussy juice. I was getting turned on by his gesture and I couldn't wait to get to his place for the main event. I drove as fast as I could to the station where his car was parked. After he got in his black Porsche, I followed behind him and we drove straight to his house.

91

When we arrived at Vinny's building, he asked me to follow him down to an underground garage where he parked his car in one spot and I parked my car next to his. He told me that both parking spots were assigned to him.

From the basement, Vinny used his key to access the elevator and we took it straight up to the top floor, but not before Vinny pinned me up against the wall and pulled my sweater up to get his sexy mouth on my delicious tities. He sucked and pulled on my nipples with his mouth like a man possessed. I had never been with a man like that in my life. While Vinny was sucking my tities, I received pain and pleasure at the same time. Every time he started pulling on them where it became painful he did something with his mouth to soothe them. I beg for his soothing touch and he delivered until the doors opened right into his suite. I didn't even have time to take inventory of his place. Everything was grand and luxurious and the whole place was decorated in earth tones. Vinny and I locked lips from the time we got off the elevator until we made our way to a staircase that led up to the roof.

Once we got to the roof, Vinny pulled his pants off and sat down on this work-out bench. All eight inches of him stood straight up. I took all my clothes off because I didn't want to get them dirty on the roof. He asked me to leave on my boots as the chill autumn air hit our bodies on the roof top. I knelt before him and I took his dick in my mouth like it a giant Vienna sausage imported straight from Italy. Vinny leaned back on the bench as he enjoyed the sensual movements of my tongue around his dick. I noticed the tip of his dick was a sensitive spot for him. While he held on to the back of my neck I licked the tip of his dick until he couldn't take it anymore. I had Vinny shaking in a trance in no time as he unleashed a good ounce of thick fluid into my mouth. I spat his cum out on his chest and rubbed it all over him. He pulled me towards him and gave me a long kiss while he stuck two of his fingers inside of me.

A few seconds later, Vinny had me leaning on the bench with my back against the part where the forty five pound weight bar along with about two hundred and fifty pounds of free weight sat. He spread my legs open wide and as they stood extended up in the air he ate my pussy like a professional. I watched Vinny stick his tongue in and out of my pussy while I held on to his head running my fingers through his thick Italian hair. He passionately ate me like it was his job to please me. He took my clit into his mouth and he twirled his tongue around it until my body started jerking and screaming the good Lord's name at the top of my lungs. As my body started to shiver, Vinny became more forceful as he held on to my legs and licked my pussy with his tongue until I couldn't take it anymore. I was still trembling when he got up and walked away to grab a towel to wipe his mouth like he had just eaten a full course meal.

While Vinny was wiping my juices off his mouth and his cum off his body, I needed a few minutes to regain myself. My pussy was so drenched in fluids I had to ask him for the towel to wipe myself as well. After wiping myself, Vinny slipped a condom on and he bent me over the bench and started smashing my ass from behind. I could feel his strokes hitting my cervix with his strong pelvic movements and the rage of a man who felt that he needed to prove himself to me because he was white. I enjoyed the way Vinny was with me when he was eating my pussy because he was genuine and he enjoyed it just as much as I did. When he started fucking me, it seemed like he had a chip on his shoulder and although his dick felt good, I didn't enjoy it as much.

I had already given in to him and he messed up the experience by trying to prove something that he didn't have to. I'm sure Vinny was a much better lover with his dick than he showed me that night, but I didn't want to be with a man who was in competition with himself and the rest of the world. When my pussy was in front of him, he should've known that it was his to take. There was no need to try to prove anything.

He should've just enjoyed the pussy the same way I wanted to enjoy his dick. Why must men always complicate things?

I left Vinny's house that night feeling unsatisfied because he didn't put his dick to good use as I expected. I went home and I took my vibrator out of the drawer to finish the job that he started. That night, I considered leaving my parents' house when I was about to reach orgasm. I wanted to scream as loud as I could but I had to hold it in because my parents were sleeping down the hall. There I was, a grown ass woman and I couldn't even enjoy the freedom of a loud orgasm the way that I wanted to. Anyway, I did come and then I went and took a shower before falling asleep flat on my back from sexual exhaustion.

The fact that the woman was a skeezer didn't even matter to me that much. I just felt betrayed by Darren and I wanted to get even.

Chapter 28

I might not have enjoyed Vinny's sexual techniques that night, but I was no fool to believe that he didn't have potential. I knew that most men have an ego and I wanted to wait until I got to know him better before I let him know that the way he tried to pierce a hole through my pussy wasn't enjoyable. As much as he would've liked for his dick to be a pleasurable drill for my pussy, I did not enjoy it, but I thought he was a cool guy. Besides, I needed to hold on to Vinny long enough to teach Darren a lesson.

I knew that Darren would feel threatened the minute he saw Vinny with me. Vinny was very good looking; he was wealthy, in shape, and smooth. I needed to use him to piss off Darren. The last thing that Darren would expect from me is to date a white guy and I knew that would set him off. I realized that night that Darren was one of those double talk brothers who walked around making people believe that Black women should be cherished and adored while he slept with White women undercover. To me those brothers are worst than the down low men. At least the men on the down low don't ostracize homosexuals unless they have to defend their parts in it.

I knew Darren was calling me every minute that night when I was with Vinny. I had my phone on vibrate and it kept going off. I never even bothered to check it. I simply turned it off when I got home and did what I had to do. As much as Darren would have liked to believe that he was a player, I wanted to show him that two could play that game. Darren forgot the one advantage that I had over him, the fact that I am female. Even if I was as ugly as King Kong and Godzilla combined, I would still have gotten more offers for dicks than he would for pussy. A lot of men would sleep with anything as long as that thing is walking around with a pussy between her legs. Being attractive with tities big enough to feed a whole village in Africa and a body most men couldn't wait to enjoy, I had the upper hand. It was up to me, however, to decide how I was going to play my game.

After he got done with his floozy, he must've been going out of his mind looking for me. Darren had the audacity to call me the next day with an attitude talking about "I was calling you all last night trying to find you and you didn't pick up your phone." I was thinking, "What nerves!" Darren was lucky that I didn't go off on him after catching him with that ugly ass woman. Before I got ahead of myself, I wanted Darren to describe to me the type of relationship we had. I asked him to define our relationship and don't you know that Negro asked me "What kind of relationship do you want it to be?" I thought to myself "okay, that's how he wants it, that's how he'll get it". I told him to leave the relationship as is and nothing more needed to be said. When he asked if I was going to spend Friday night with him, I simply responded, "I've got plans".

I knew he was fuming inside because Darren was not used to being second in my life. I had always put him first and I thought it was understood that after we graduated from college we were going to get back together. I was obviously wrong and I didn't want him to assume that he was right. I told Darren exactly where I was going and who I was going to be with. When he asked, "where did you meet this guy?" I was happy to tell him that I met Vinny at the same place where he was kissing his skeezer girlfriend in the VIP section. I was waiting for his reaction because Darren knew that I had solid information on him.

He wasn't a convincing liar, so he didn't even try to lie his way out of it, but he wasn't totally honest about the situation either. He fumbled around it until I told him to forget it and that he did not owe me an explanation. Darren always hated it when I ended our conversation with an open-ended statement. He was busted and he knew it and now the ball was in my court, but unlike Darren, I wanted him to know exactly what I was doing.

In the past, Darren would always call me after he got home from the club just to tell me that he made it home. On the few occasions that he didn't call me, I suspected it was because he probably brought home one of his skeezers. He thought he was so slick by making me believe that he was just hanging out with his buddies. I didn't even see any of his co-workers around him when he was with that woman. That place must've been his special pick-up spot. I had it in for Darren and I made sure he knew it. I was about to unleash a new game on him that he never expected from me.

Chapter 29

That Friday evening I wore the sexiest little red dress for my date with Vinny. I purposely stopped by Darren's house to pick up my matching red purse that I had left there. He couldn't believe his eyes when he saw me. I looked like a woman who was ready to be ordered, served and eaten by one lucky man or maybe even two. I could see that he wanted to say something about my dress, but he didn't because he didn't want to give me more ammunition. I simply walked in, grabbed my purse from his closet and then I left.

I had noticed a drastic change in Darren's attitude after he got his own place. He wasn't spending as much time with me anymore. When he lived at home with his parents, I saw him almost everyday. He was never tired of being around me. Even my parents wondered if he was suffocating me. I guess, with his own place, came newfound freedom. I was looking for that kind of freedom myself. I couldn't wait for Darren to move into his new condo. I was more excited than him. We were finally going to have the freedom that we wanted to do everything sexually imaginable. However, I was disappointed to learn that he was looking forward to banging a lot more other chicks than me. I had bought a lot of special lingerie, special sex toys and body oils just to please him at his new place. I was even angrier because I couldn't even enjoy a good masturbating session at home. Letting him see me looking as sexy as I wanted to be was part of my little revenge.

Darren had no idea that Vinny was outside waiting for me in his Porsche when I went to pick up my purse. When he offered to walk me to my car, I told him that I was not driving and that my date had brought me by his house to pick up my purse. He was livid when he learned that I had brought another man by his house. I left his apartment feeling vindicated and happy. As I made my way back towards Vinny's car, he got out from his side to open the passenger door for me and I knew that Darren was probably watching from his living room window. I wanted to laugh out loud, but I didn't want to appear crazy to Vinny. I never told Vinny that I was going to Darren's house. I lied to him. I told him I was stopping by my girlfriend's to pick up a purse that she had borrowed. I knew Darren well enough to know that he would never get into any kind of physical altercation or confrontation with another man unless I was being disrespected, but it was still a gamble, a gamble that paid off in a big way.

I really don't understand why men never want to show appreciation for their women until somebody else starts to show interest in her. Women are sometimes like that as well and I don't understand them either. I wanted Darren to know that there were other men out there that were interested in me and if he didn't step up to the plate, I could be gone. I think he got the message because he kept calling me the whole night and leaving text messages on my cell phone telling me that we need to talk about our relationship. I specifically chose to spend the night over Vinny's house that night because I knew Darren would drive by my parents' house to make sure I came straight home from my date.

Even though I had a great time with Vinny that night eating at a five star restaurant, Darren still dominated my every thought. There was something about Darren that was so magnetic, no other man could ever take my mind off him. Even when I was butt naked in Vinny's hot tub with my legs spread wide open across his arms while he ate my pussy, I still imagined the touch of Darren's hands and the sweetness of his voice telling me how much he cared about me. I didn't even cum that night when I was with Vinny. I was preoccupied with Darren and Vinny didn't notice a thing.

Vinny was either too selfish to know that I was not into the sex or he just didn't give a damn. Either way, that was going to be our last outing. Vinny was a great guy in many ways, but he just wasn't my kind of guy. I felt kind of weird when I was out with Vinny as well. Too many people were staring at us. I didn't know if people stared because I was wearing a banging dress that accentuated my curves, or if they found it odd that such a good looking White boy was out with a Black woman. The White women especially had their eyes piercing right through me to read Vinny's body language.

The Black people were just blatant with their shit. One brother just screamed at the top of his lung "The brothers ain't good enough for ya!" I told Vinny to ignore him because I saw his Italian machismo was about to come out to confront the guy. There was this sister in dreads who just stared right at me until I was too embarrassed to look her in the eyes anymore. I wondered why people still made a big deal of interracial couples. As much as we would like to believe that America is a melting pot, there's about a million people waiting to halt that progress or process. I'm not sure if it's really progress when people of different racial and ethnic backgrounds go out together.

I didn't decide to stop going out with Vinny because of all the nasty looks and stares that I received from both Black and White people. I stopped seeing him because I wasn't that much into him and my heart was with Darren. Vinny had been calling me and I didn't return his calls. He thought it was because other people made me feel uncomfortable with him. It was going to be hard to explain to him that I was using him to make Darren jealous, so I decided to just tell him that I was getting back with my ex-boyfriend because he wanted another chance.

Chapter 30

It turned out that Vinny wasn't such a nice guy after all. He became a pain in the ass and a stalker. It seemed like Vinny was so used to getting everything that he wanted, he didn't know how to deal with the word "no". He continued to call me leaving threatening messages on my phone telling me that if I thought I could use him and then leave him I had something coming. I never had a stalker in my life and I didn't know how serious Vinny's threats were. I took it very lightly and I thought he was just momentarily pissed because his ego was bruised and he would get over it in due time. I couldn't be more wrong.

As time went by, I started going out with this other guy. I wasn't ready to run back to Darren just yet. I wanted to have my fun and make him pay in the process. I met Phillip Thompson when I went to this job site to make sure things were going according to plan for my father. Phil was a young engineer on the site who was aggressive and eager to get as much of his work done as soon as he could; he turned me on almost right away. He was about five feet ten inches tall with a slim build, light skin with very light brown eyes and a little bowlegged. His walk alone had my panties dripping wet, but when he smiled after we were introduced, I almost melted. I knew that I had to have Phil because that man was just too sexy to overlook. I spent all day at the job site doing nothing more than what my father asked me to do. I was waiting for the right opportunity at the end of the day to talk to Phil. I wanted to set a good example in front of the other workers. I didn't want to waste company time talking to Phil while he was on the job.

Five o'clock had finally come and everybody was headed home at the end of a long day of hard work. I asked Phil if he had a few minutes because I needed to talk to him in the office. My father had these makeshift trailer offices at every job site in case he needed to do some paperwork or have meetings with his clients. I could see that Phil was a little intimidated by my request. I could tell that Phil was worried that he was going to be scolded for something related to his job. I immediately put his mind at ease when I told him it had nothing to do with his job performance. I watched his face and it looked like a big burden had been lifted off his shoulders. I didn't know why he was worried so much at first, but after he told me that he was going to take his briefcase to his car and that he'd be back momentarily, I knew why he was so worried. Phil was probably earning about forty to forty five thousand dollars with the company, but he was driving a fifty thousand dollar Cadillac, Escalade truck. I'd be worried about my job too if I were him.

Why he was driving such an expensive car, I don't know. I don't understand why these men try so hard to keep up with the joneses by living beyond their means. It's always nice to dream big, but sometimes we have to pace ourselves so we don't get ahead of ourselves. Phil seemed ambitious and determined enough to me to move up the ranks within the company in no time, but I didn't understand his reasons for owning such an expensive car while his salary could hardly help him keep up with the payments. It was none of my business and the only thing I cared about was whether or not he could lay the pipe like a good plumber.

By the time Phil came back to the office to meet me, the coast was clear and everybody had gone home. I noticed that it was always hard to get the employees to start work in the morning, but when five o'clock came, they vanished like water in a dry desert in Africa. When Phil walked into the office, I offered him a bottle of water. I figured he was thirsty from being out in the sun all day working. He took the bottle of water from me and took it to the head in one take. "Somebody was thirsty," I said. He didn't say anything back.

I didn't know why, but I woke up that morning feeling feminine and sexy, so I decided to wear a tan skirt to work with a white blouse and my tan three-inch heel pointed shoes. I usually kept a pair of construction boots in the trunk of my car for when I visit the jobsites. When Phil and I met earlier, I was wearing my construction boots and my blouse was buttoned almost all the way up to my neck. However, when he came to my office, I had time to freshen up in the bathroom, I took off my boots and wore my tan shoes and loosened a couple of the buttons on my blouse exposing a little cleavage.

The sweet scent of my perfume was still fresh and I could tell that Phil was enthralled by the aroma of the chemical reaction that my body created with the perfume. The little slit on my skirt was also shifted from the back to the front near my inner thighs. It was just more convenient for me to have it that way. I sat on the edge of the desk while Phil took a seat in the chair in front of me. His face and my breasts were at eyelevel and I made sure I bent down after every sentence so I could peak Phil's interest. I asked him if he was married or had any children and Phil told me "no". That pretty much left the door open for anything and I was hungry for a piece of Phil-e-mignon. I positioned myself in front of Phil in a way so that the slit in the front of my skirt would open wide enough for him to see my white silk thong underwear.

He wasn't as aggressive as I wanted him to be with me. I wished he would use the same aggression that he used in his job with me, but to no avail. I needed to make the first move, but I wanted to be cautious because the last thing I wanted to bring to my parents was a sexual harassment suit by a nice, sexy looking young man who worked for the company. After wasting too much time on small talk with Phil, I asked him if he was intimidated by me or women in powerful positions in general. He all of sudden got manly on me and told me "No woman can intimidate me. I'm very secure as a man and I always take the lead when I need to". I wished I never asked that question because he sounded too stupid to even take seriously, but he was still handsome and sexy.

I asked him another casual question just to get his reaction, "if I told you that you could do anything that you wanted to me right now, what's the first thing you would do?" He paused for a moment then asked, "Do you want me to be honest?" "Sure, speak your mind" I said. Phil pulled his eyes up from my tities and looked straight in my eyes and told me "I would lick the hell out of your pussy, take your tities in my mouth, lean your ass back against the desk and fuck the hell out of you." "What are you waiting for?" I asked.

Phil slowly unbuttoned the last few buttons on my blouse, he pulled my tities out of my bra and took one of them in his mouth while he caressed the other one with his hand. I decided to help him out a little by unclasping my bra myself. He had two huge double D breasts at his disposal and he was sucking away. Phil brought my nipples together in his mouth and he started sucking on them just long enough to get them erected and my pussy running wet like a wild river.

I reached for his crotch and I found a hard seven inch dick that I didn't believe was going to do much damage to my pussy. I was a little disappointed that he didn't have a bigger dick, but I would later find out that sometimes it's "the motion of the ocean and not the size of the boat that mattered" as I used to hear it when I was in high school. Phil started kissing me and he was one of the best kissers that I had ever kissed. His lips were full and thick and his tongue was soft and smooth. He extended his tongue out of his mouth while he was kissing me and I sucked on it like it was an erect dick. He sucked on my tongue as well and from the way he kissed me, I was convinced that he knew how to deliver the kind of oral stimulation that a sister needed at the time. Phil made his way back down to my tits and started kissing and caressing them with his hands and mouth. Meanwhile, I was trembling and my juices started running down my thighs through my underwear. By the time Phil made his way down to my navel with his tongue, I had my head tilted back waiting for his tongue to wander around my crotch area.

He pulled my skirt up above my thighs and pulled my underwear to the side with his finger and he started eating me as I leaned back against the desk holding on to the edges in case my knees gave in. Phil ate me using techniques that I would later use in my own personal relationship with another woman. He held my clit inside his mouth in a tight grip with his lips wrapped around it while he used his tongue in a circular motion to lick me. My clit stood erected in his mouth until I had to grab on to his neck and almost squeezed the fucking life out of him while I came. Phil didn't even allow my orgasm to completely run through me before he wrapped himself in a condom and stuck his dick inside of me. In mid-orgasm, he stuck his dick inside my pussy and I was on fire. He leaned my leg up against his chest as he damn near inserted his balls inside of me with every stroke. His technique was something that I had never seen and I felt every inch of him inside of me.

After I came over and over on the table from the thrusting of Phil's dick and the stimulation of my clit at his fingers, he had me lie down on my stomach with my torso laying on the desk and my legs hanging off the table while he pummeled my pussy from behind. He held on to my legs and fucked the hell out of me until I couldn't come any more. I noticed that Phil never came while he was fucking me and when I asked him why, he told me because he was waiting to come in my mouth. I was tired and worn out, but I pulled his condom off and I took his seven inch dick inside my mouth like a Subway sandwich. I sucked his dick until he screamed for mercy and came all over my chest.

Chapter 31

Phil was exactly what I needed until I was ready to make up my mind on whether or not I wanted to patch things up with Darren. But Vinny wouldn't allow nature to take its course so smoothly. One night while I was out with Phil in Manhattan, Vinny pulled up next to us as we walked holding hands and screamed "That's the little punk that you ran back to!" Vinny was significantly bigger than Phil, but Phil was no punk and he wasn't going to let some Wall Street tough-guy wannabe call him out without saying anything. Phil answered, "Why don't you pull your car over so I can show your bitch ass who's really a punk, chump!" Thank goodness there was no where for Vinny to pull over because the traffic was crazy that night on Thirty Fourth Street. I begged Phil to let it go and I had to explain to him that Vinny was someone that I only went out with a couple of times and he didn't know how to let go and move on.

I was walking a fine line with Phil because I didn't really want him to use his job to manipulate the "sexual relation-ship" that we had. I had not told my parents that I was mess-ing around with any of the employees and I also didn't want Phil to start pulling rank at the job site because he was fuck-ing the boss' daughter. The good times were rolling with Phil, but over time I started to notice that he was asking me to pay for our outings more and more. I clearly understood that Phil was not earning that much money, but I'm from the old school with a little twist of the modern world and I believe that a man should be able to treat a lady occasionally. I wasn't look-ing for him to pay every time we went out, but if he thought I was going to be treating him to the most expensive restau-rants in town all the time, he had something coming.

Phil was confident that he knew how to swing that dick, but he thought he could use that to try to act like a gigolo with me. He must not have gotten the memo that I sent out to tell people "I have had quite a few good dicks in my life and none was good enough to make me act foolishly". I would've given him more credit if he went about it in a different way, but I could see right through him. For some reason, he thought that he was macking me and never once realized that I was the macker from the beginning. Whenever we were going out and I was treating, Phil would only mention five star restaurants like I was his ATM machine or something. But whenever he offered to treat me to a meal, it was always BBQ's, Chili's and Fridays. I don't think we ever ate at any place where the bill came to more than twenty five dollars when he had to pay. I admit that I took him to a couple of five star restaurants, but it was because I wanted to try the food myself and he was always good company. I was in on his game, but I didn't say anything.

My plan for the next few weeks was to convince Phil that there wasn't much room for advancement in my father's company because all the people who had been working there didn't plan on going anywhere. I painted a bleak picture of a future for him and he bought into it. One of the reasons I wanted Phil to leave the company was because I didn't want him to sue my dad after I dropped his ass. Phil was good at his job, but my father always told me that everyone who ever worked for him was expendable. "The minute a person starts to believe that they're so good at their job that no one could replace them, you have to make them believe that's not so," He'd say. It wasn't that my father wasn't loyal to his employees, but he didn't want anybody dictating to him how he should run his company. Everyone received their fair market value and he was fair and honest with them. I tried as much as I could to absorb the business lessons that my dad was trying to teach me.

It didn't take me long to figure out that Phil was a manipulative person who would use any situation to his advantage.

My plan was to beat him to the punch. Phil was driving an Escalade because he had women paying his bills for him. His phone was always ringing and he could never talk when I was around. As fine as he was, I knew that I wasn't the only woman who fell for his good looks and his excellent bedroom skills. He might've thought that he was using me, but I wore his little seven inch dick out until I got sick of it. The nerve of him to think that he was gonna control me with his dick. He had skills, but he didn't have the kind of dick that would make me go goo-goo gaga over him. I have always had emotional pussy control. I made sure I took control of my emotions when it came to sex with men. I never stressed anything about any man. The only men that I can honestly say I would give my life for are my brother and my dad. Not even Darren has earned that honor yet.

I was able to help Phil research a few construction firms and he landed a job that paid him fifty thousand dollars, which was five thousand dollars more than my father's company was paying him. I urged him to take the job and I gave him a great recommendation. When he handed his resignation in to my dad, my dad was very surprised. He couldn't understand why Phil was leaving his company all of a sudden. He was even willing to offer Phil more money, but my manipulative ways had gotten the best of Phil and he was out the door. After all, my dad did say that everyone was expendable. It was time for him to expand himself and find a new replacement for Phil and if I had anything to do with it, it would be a married man that I wasn't attracted to at all.

Chapter 32

Darren continued to call me and we talked about our problems without ever coming up with a solution. I still cared for him and I wanted to be with him, but he wasn't ready to settle down with one girlfriend just yet and I was having my own little fun on the side, anyway. I told Darren that he needed to be honest with himself. "You're right. I need more time to myself to get acclimated in my new condo apartment, but you are more than welcome to call me anytime when ever you need something. Especially for a booty call" he said, smiling. Darren had a way of saying offensive things to me without offending me. We were only in our mid-twenties and had only been out of college for about a year. So, I told him to take as much time as he needed to do his thing, but there was no promise that I would still be available when he was ready to come back to me.

I was happy to patch things up with Darren. We were becoming friends once again and I also told him about the ugly white girl that I saw him with that night at Cheetah's. He was surprised to hear that I was even in the club. "My hope was to surprise you, but I ended up being the surprised one" I said, laughing. We could joke about it afterwards, but at the time I was seriously angry with him for lying to me. I'm not saying that I've always been totally forthcoming with Darren, but he has yet to catch me in a situation or a lie. The saying that "women are better cheaters and liars than men" has to have some type of credibility because Darren totally trusted me and I played my games right.

Because I used an open dialogue policy with Darren, he trusted that I was totally honest with him about everything that went on in my life. I didn't do things in a sneaky way like he did. I told him exactly what I was gonna do and who I was gonna do it with. Darren however, would try to take my sincerity for granted. Whenever he started asking for details about my encounters with other men, I found a way to change the subject. Like most men, if Darren knew that I was sleeping with so many men, he would have lost respect for me and he would've thought that I was a whore. The way I was able to keep him from thinking that way about me, was to supply him with as much pussy as he wanted whenever he wanted it. His pussy demands were always a priority because he was the only man that could completely satisfy me sexually. Darren and I fucked so much and so often there was no way that he thought that I had enough energy left in me to fuck with other men.

If Darren called me while I was out with another man and wanted me to come over to be with him, I would make up an excuse to get away from that man. I understood his psyche and I was able to play right along to what he wanted me to be. I knew that Darren was possibly out there looking for a better prospect, but I never denied him anything and he never had enough time on his hands to spend with a woman to allow himself to get close enough to her to be pulled away from me. I already knew that I was satisfied with Darren, but I didn't want to be sitting at home waiting for him, I wanted to enjoy my life as well. After He and I were on good terms, I never spent the night out with any other man. Even after I got my own place, I didn't allow any men other than Darren to stay over because I was aware of his bad habits of dropping by my house unannounced. Giving him a key was out of the question because he had refused to give me his house keys in return when the subject was discussed.

He had total and complete access to me however, and felt very secure about that. I also made it a rule not to sleep with any of my dates until after I talked to Darren on that day. I needed to make sure that I wasn't going to have sex with Darren on any specific day before I slept with another man. I never really wanted to sleep with two different men in one day. However, my fantasy was to be with two men at one time. Don't get me wrong, I was still out there sleeping with plenty of guys, but Darren would never think that because I made him believe that my pussy belonged to him. Another thing that I didn't do was to date men who lived near me or near Darren. I never wanted any of my men to cross paths, but psychotic Vinny would prove that theory wrong once again.

Chapter 33

After accepting his new position at a new construction company, I decided to take Phil out to this nice restaurant to celebrate. I was really celebrating myself because I was finally getting rid of Phil for good. He was on his way to start a new job and there was no way he could sue the company for sexual harassment. There was this little Italian restaurant that I really liked in Manhattan that everybody else in New York City seemed to like as well. The place was always booked and a reservation was needed to eat there every time. Vinny knew it was my favorite restaurant because he took me there once. It had been a few months and he was still calling me and I never returned his phone calls. I never realized what the words "pussy whipped" meant until I met Vinny. This guy was in love with my pussy for some reason and I just never understood why. As good looking as Vinny was, he could've gotten with a number of fine women. Why was he so stuck on me? I wondered.

To celebrate that evening, I had decided to call my favorite restaurant earlier in the day to make a reservation for two, but I didn't know that Vinny had been frequenting that restaurant almost every weekend hoping to catch me there with my "boyfriend". He was on a first name basis with the staff and owner there after a while. The restaurant believed that they had a lifetime client in Vinny because their food was good. It turned out that their food had nothing to do with Vinny's presence at the restaurant all the time. I hadn't gone to the restaurant because I was spending most of my time with Darren and this other guy that I was messing with who's not even worth mentioning. His dick was totally garbage and I wasted my time with him. I even tried to teach the bastard a thing or two so he could use that big ass dick that God blessed him with, but he just couldn't do it. It was a nice piece of dick gone to waste.

Anyway, when Phil and I entered the restaurant, I didn't even notice Vinny sitting on the corner looking out for us. He had his face hidden behind the menu and I sat with my back to him. Phil was too busy talking about himself telling me how he had planned to become a manager at his new job in the next year, to even notice Vinny watching us from the back corner. We sat in the restaurant for almost two hours eating and drinking and planning to go back to Phil's house for a last and final parting fuck from him. Darren had gone to Atlantic City with his boys and I knew he wasn't coming back until the next morning. I was planning on staying at Phil's house until the wee hours of the morning fucking his brains out.

After filling up our stomachs with some wonderful culinary dishes and treats at my favorite restaurant, Phil and I got up to leave to go back to his house. We went outside and handed the valet the ticket for my car, but before the valet had a chance to return with my car, Vinny showed up and he bumped and shoved Phil to the ground. Of course, I expected Phil to get up from the ground and charge at Vinny, but I begged him not to fight him. Vinny thought he could teach Phil a lesson for taking his "woman" from him. Phil stood up and they were now facing each other in a guarded position. Vinny was one of those fearless guys who threw a bunch of wild punches with his head down. He connected once on his first slew of punches, then Phil stepped back to watch his fighting style. Before Vinny could go on the attack again, Phil set him up with a right hook and before I knew it, Phil hit Vinny with an uppercut that sent him to the pavement, lying flat on his back in front of the restaurant.

The situation was embarrassing for all of us as all the people at the restaurant stopped in the middle of their meals to come to the window to watch Phil and Vinny fight. It was more like to watch Vinny get his ass whipped. By the time Vinny came to, Phil was talking much shit and he was ready to

113

knock Vinny out again. The owner and the staff at the restaurant came outside to break up the fight and promised to call the cops if they continued. By then, the valet had brought my car back and I asked Phil to get in while a few guys held Vinny back. I took off very quickly and I made sure that Vinny wasn't following me in the rearview mirror.

I was a little frightened by Vinny's actions and I wondered if I should go to the police the following Monday to get a restraining order against him. I spoke about it with Phil and he assured me that Vinny wouldn't be coming back to bother me again because his pride was shattered and he most likely wouldn't want to face me again. The only other thing I thought about while I was in the car with Phil was "Thank goodness it wasn't Darren". Because Darren would've made sure that Vinny didn't come after me ever again. Vinny would have certainly ended up in the hospital for days.

The scuffle between Vinny and Phil almost took away my sexual desires to have Phil tie me up to his canopy bed like he promised earlier on our way to the restaurant. However, as he reached over and started massaging my inner thighs in the car, again, I started imagining myself tied up to his bedpost and him having his way with me. When we got to Phil's house, he picked me up and took me straight to his bedroom. He pulled out a stack of ties and he started tying me down one leg and arm at a time until I laid flat on my back across his bed. Phil even went a step further when he took one of his ties and blindfolded me. The mysterious mood kept me in total anticipation of a gratifying sexual moment. I had not done anything like that with Phil in the past, but I knew that he had never disappointed me.

Moments after I was blindfolded, I could feel a warm liquid being poured over my body and it smelled like cherry. After Phil poured the liquid all over my body, he proceeded to give me a rub-down. The motion of his hands on my body was very sensual and he massaged every crevice on my body. It felt even better when he made his way down to my crotch and he started massaging my clit with his fingers. He pulled the skin back on my clit and started slowly caressing it with one finger at a time. Phil kept talking to me and asking me if I liked it because there was more. I could only say "Bring it on, Papi" like I was Puerto Rican.

Phil left and came back a few minutes later with a cold substance this time and he poured a small scoop on each of my breast and an even smaller scoop on my clit. After he placed his mouth on my nipples and started licking me, I figured he had poured ice cream on me. He worked his tongue and the ice cream on my breasts until he consumed both of them. Then, he went down to my pussy and started licking my clit ala ice cream until my body gave in to his tongue and I exclaimed "I'm coming!"

Phil wasn't done with me yet. He untied me then flipped me over on my stomach. He took a washcloth and he wiped down my ass and my pussy clean. He again poured the cold ice cream on the crack of my ass and he started licking my asshole until I begged him to stop because I couldn't take it anymore. Phil was out to conquer me and he was pulling all the stunts to do it. No man had ever licked my ass before and when Phil asked if I ever had a rim job done to me before, I was dumbfounded because I didn't know what the hell he was talking about. He then said "allow me to demonstrate once again". He poured more ice cream on my ass crack and he proceeded to lick my asshole and my pussy simultaneously until I begged him to stop again. That shit was heavenly, but I didn't want to be tied up while he did it.

It was enough with the licking. Phil wanted to take me from the back, so he untied my legs and asked me to raise my ass up to penetrate me from behind. I could feel the contour of his dick thrusting in and out of me slowly as he took his index finger and stuck it in my ass. At one point I didn't know which felt better, his dick or his finger in my ass. I was being pleased in every which way and Phil knew it. While he was pummeling my ass from behind with his finger in my asshole,

I came over and over. After I was done, he pulled his condom off and he masturbated over my ass until he came and splattered all his semen all over my rear end. Afterwards, Phil untied my hands and took the blindfold off my eyes then he handed me a towel to clean myself. I could see the smirk on his face because he knew that he had put it on me and it was a matter of time before he had this rich little girl start spending daddy's money on him. I always stayed a step ahead of the men that I dealt with and I knew exactly where Phil was going with his game. He was good, but not good enough to think that he could mack me.

Chapter 34

I left Phil's house that morning feeling completely satisfied, but I was still paranoid about Vinny. I kept looking in my rearview mirror to find him. I knew that he didn't know where I lived because I had not spoken to him since I moved into my new house, but one can never be too cautious. When I arrived at my house, I proceeded with caution and I made sure that the coast was clear. After the garage door closed behind me, I went inside the house and checked every room to make sure that no one was there. I didn't want Vinny's crazy ass to catch me off guard.

Completely exhausted, I hopped in my bed and I went to sleep until three o'clock the next day. Even though Phil did all of the work the night before, his tactics however, wore me out and I needed to rest before I saw Darren. I knew that Darren was going be looking to get some ass from me and I wanted to be prepared. I didn't even realize that Darren had called me around noon. I was knocked the hell out. He called me back at three pm that afternoon and I awoke to his phone call. Darren hadn't seen me in a couple of days and he wanted us to do something nice together. Since the weather was nice on that Saturday, I suggested that we go to Broadway to check out Bring the Noise, Bring the Funk, starring Savion Glover. I had this new little cocktail dress that I was looking forward to wearing and Darren presented me with the opportunity.

Darren came to my place to pick me up at seven thirty on the dot, I wasn't completely ready, but I was ninety nine percent there. His eyes lit up when I opened the door and he saw my dress and of course he had to pull me close to him for a kiss while he copped a feel of my round derriere. We drove straight to Manhattan and we parked in this parking lot that wasn't too far from the theatre. That evening, I felt paranoid the whole time I was with Darren. I kept wondering if Vinny had followed us to the theatre and I was hoping he didn't try to confront Darren like he did Phil.

Darren didn't mess around and I knew that Vinny wouldn't stand a chance against Darren after seeing how easily Phil knocked his ass to the ground. I could tell that Darren was a little annoyed with me because I kept looking behind me and around me. He finally asked if something was wrong and I lied and told him that my neck was hurting because I slept on one side of my neck the previous night and I had to keep turning so it wouldn't lock up on me. I was good with my lies.

Darren and I enjoyed watching Savion Glover's unshaven self tap his ass into the white people's hearts. The man is really talented, but he could use a shave every now and then. After we left Broadway, Darren suggested that we go to my favorite restaurant where the incident took place with Phil and Vinny. I quickly diverted his attention to somewhere else, as I told him that I was not in the mood for Italian food. That night I decided to eat soul food because I didn't want to go back to that restaurant for at least a good year. I was embarrassed by Vinny and Phil and there was no way I was gonna walk in there with Darren and have the whole staff at the place stare at me.

Since I lied to Darren and told him that I was in the mood for soul food, he decided that we should walk to Motown Café right in the heart of Manhattan. The place is no longer open today, but when it was open, Darren and I used to go there all the time for soul food and it was a beautiful restaurant. We walked into Motown Café and I was still paranoid. I looked in every corner to make sure that Vinny wasn't in the place waiting for me. I didn't know if he had hired a private investigator to tell him my whereabouts and I didn't want him springing up on me from out of nowhere.

It took a little time before we were finally seated, but the couple of drinks that I had at the bar while we waited for our table, calmed my nerves a little. I was not as paranoid and I started to relax a little. The waitress came by and took our order and Darren and I talked about what we did the previous night. Of course, I lied and told him that I went out with a new guy that I was not into at all. He started telling me about his great night at the Blackjack table and how he walked away a winner with almost two thousand dollars. And since he mentioned that he won so much money, I playfully asked him to pay for dinner. He told me that he already knew that dinner was on him, but I was just playing.

One of the things that I liked about Darren was the fact that he never tried to take advantage of me because of my fortunate background. He always offered to pay when we went out and he always treated me like lady. If I could build the perfect man, ninety percent of him would comprise of Darren. There was so much that I liked about him, I just knew that I couldn't let another woman have him. I set him free because if he truly belonged to me, he would come back on his own, but Darren never completely left, anyway. He always had one foot in the door. I think he wanted to make sure that I didn't go anywhere either.

All through dinner Darren kept rubbing my knees under table and making his presence felt. He even took one of his shoes off and started rubbing his toe on my crotch getting me excited. It was almost like he could feel my excited clitoris with his toe. He started rubbing it through my thong underwear and before I knew it my pussy was all wet. He just knew that we were gonna go home after dinner and tear each other up. As good as Phil made me feel the night before, I welcomed the sensual touch of Darren's hands all over my body.

While I masticated on barbequed ribs, collard greens and mashed potatoes, I was running my foot up and down Darren's legs under table until I got a rise out of him. When I moved my toe near his crotch and felt the bulge in his pants,

I just smiled at him and he knew exactly what I meant. Darren was the only guy that ever made me feel sexy all the time. Don't get me wrong, I knew I was wanted by these other men that I slept with, but Darren brought out my sex appeal and confidence. I could be in a room full of people with Darren and his eyes would be fixated on me. I couldn't wait to get home to rip his clothes off and tear him to shreds.

As I smiled at Darren's gestures underneath the table, he was about to make the boldest move yet. Darren dropped his cloth napkin on the floor and I knew what was coming next. Since our table was in the corner of the restaurant, Darren was able to position himself under the table to eat me until I started marinating in my own juices. It was so hard for me to keep a straight face while he ate my pussy. I kept fighting my eyelids from closing as he forced me to climax right in the restaurant in front of a bunch of people. Although no one noticed when he went under the table, the waitress however, was standing right there when he came up wiping his mouth and I could pretty much sense that she knew what was going on. She may have caught me shaking a little bit when she got to the table. Darren was going to get it when we got home and he was going to get it good!

After Darren paid the bill, we rushed out of the restaurant laughing our asses off. That shit was so exhilarating because I never expected it from Darren. We took a long trek back to the parking lot walking hand in hand. I didn't care about Vinny showing up anymore. I knew that Darren could handle himself and he would protect me with his life if he had to. When we got to the parking lot, we jumped in the car and drove straight to Darren's house. But I couldn't help myself in the car; I had to get a little dessert before we reached his house. I took Darren's dick in my mouth from the time he got on the Long Island Express way, all the way to his house. Darren's dick was rock hard and I couldn't wait to have it inside of me.

When Darren finally got through opening his front door with much interruption from me trying to feel every inch of his body, he pushed the door behind him and he lifted my dress up, picked me up from the floor and pinned me up against the wall and he just took his dick and shoved it inside my pussy with voracity and desperation. I wrapped my legs around his body as he banged away at my pussy until sweat started pouring all over him from the strain of my weight. After pounding me for a few minutes while he held me up against the wall, he turned me around to face the wall while he fucked me from behind. I was starting to sweat myself, so I pulled my dress up over my head to allow my body a little ventilation. While Darren stroked me from behind, he squeezed my tities and pulled on my nipples making me hotter and hotter.

Darren had this thing that he used to do whenever he fucked me from the back and I always came when he did it. I saw him lowering himself down so he could give me his longest strokes and I knew that I would be coming any minute. Darren was able to do a lot of things to me because he had a long dick. A man with a short penis wouldn't have the kind of distance between his dick and my pussy that Darren had. With the tip of his dick barely inside me, Darren started stroking me from a bended knee position all the way up to a full stand. He was killing my pussy and I just kept coming and coming and I knew that he was about to come too because he held on to me tight as he delivered his last stroke. We just stood there against the wall as he wrapped his hands around my body to tell me how much he cared about me. And that's another good reason why I always felt so safe in Darren's arms.

Chapter 35

After that great night of passionate sex and fun with Darren, we decided that we were going to be exclusive with each other. Of course, that meant that I had to get rid of Phil and everybody else who was calling me. I had never told Darren about Phil or Vinny. I always made up a name whenever I told him I was going out with a guy. He figured that I was trying to use these men to keep me company when he couldn't be with me. I never asked him, but I didn't think that Darren thought I was sleeping with any other men besides him. And that's just the way I wanted it to be. What he didn't know wouldn't hurt him.

It was easy for me to keep a couple of lame guys that I had brief encounters with from calling me. They somehow believed that they had a permanent chance with me. I really don't understand men sometimes. There were these two knuckleheads that I tried to sleep with at different times, of course. They both climaxed at the touch of my hands on their dicks like they were teenagers. And for some reason they believed that I would call them again for a second round. We never had a first round to begin with. What is it that they didn't get? These premies came before my bra even came off of me. They weren't even "minute men" I called them "seconds men". The fact that I never returned their phone calls should have been the biggest clue that I was through with them, but no! They just didn't get it. They were some fine ass men too.

Anyway, I decided to pick up the phone one day to set one of them straight. He was all excited when he heard my voice. He was trying to be smooth, calling me "sweet angel" and shit. The time that he should've gotten smooth was when I was willing to give him some pussy. Instead, he never even got near my pussy because he was a preemie at the age of thirty. I had to cut his rant off to tell him that I didn't want him to call me anymore. Don't you know this motherfucker had the nerves to ask me, why? I almost crushed his ego with the obvious, but I took the long road instead by telling him that I was involved with someone and that it was serious. That was the end of my statement before I hung up the phone. There was really nothing more to talk about.

The second guy pretty much was about to dish out the same mumbo jumbo, but I didn't even give him a chance to do it. I cut him off and told him that I didn't want him to call me anymore because I wasn't interested. I know what I did was rude, but I was pissed for wasting my time with them. By the time a man reaches a certain age, he should be exempt from certain limitations. You can not come all over yourself at the touch of a woman's hand when you're thirty years old, maybe a thirteen year-old, I can understand.

It was easy for me to get rid of those two bums, but getting rid of Phil brought a surprise of its own. I called Phil and made an appointment with him to tell him that we needed to talk because I had something important that I wanted to tell him. On the day of our meeting, I left straight from work to go to his house. By then it was habitual for me to check my rearview mirror for Vinny. I never noticed any black Porsches behind me and I thought I was safe. I drove straight to Phil's house and we sat in his living room and I told him that I couldn't see him anymore. Yes, he was a little upset with me for ending everything so abruptly, but I had already made up my mind that I wanted to be with Darren and only Darren.

Phil didn't even want to hug me goodbye. In a way, I think that he was crushed because his plan to woo me didn't work and he was never going to have me in the palm of his hands like he had planned. Phil never factored in that I had my own plans and his sexual skills and prowess were good to me for as long as I wanted him, not because I needed him. This might sound callous and cold, but I wanted to use Phil because he thought his dick was his most powerful possession. Most guys who looked as good as Phil would try to capitalize on their good looks by dating women with self esteem issues, but I give Phil credit because he wasn't like that. He went about it a different way and I'm sure that he was successful with it in the past with a couple of dumb broads.

While I was at his house one day, I opened his closet door when he was in the shower and I noticed all kinds of gift items still wrapped and pictures of a bunch of beautiful women posing in front of big mansions, Rolls Royce, Mercedes and wearing the best high fashion that money can buy. Phil wore many different watches when we went out. He had a Movado, Rolex, Cartier and Tag Huer and I knew they were all gifts that he received from other women. Many of the cards that he received were sexually explicit and the women were always telling him that they couldn't get enough of him. Phil was a certified gigolo who was up against a "Gigolette". I know that Gigolette is not a word goddamn it, but I needed to say that he met his female match with emphasis.

I was actually a little sad after I broke it off with Phil. I really enjoyed being with him and he was a fun guy to be around. They say that "all good things must come to end" and Phil was one of those things that I had to end. He was no good for me and I knew it, but the allure of a bad boy got the best of me because I cared for him a lot. Phil was the type of guy that most women would want to try to change because he was so good at what he did. However, I was looking to the future and Phil couldn't be tamed even if I had Halle Berry's money and looks.

Chapter 36

I arrived home from Phil's house and the first thing I did was turn on my television in the family room to the local news channel. I went to the kitchen to get a glass of water before I kicked my shoes off to lounge on the sofa. While I was in the fridge pouring out the water, I heard the anchor woman talking about a man who was found beaten to death in Hempstead, Long Island. That little part of the news drew my attention instantly. I left the fridge open and the glass of water on the counter to run back to the television.

Hempstead made me think of Phil immediately because that's where he lived. To my disappointment, it was Phil who was found murdered in his house, beaten savagely to death with a bat by an assailant. I knew for certain it was him because the police lines were circling the front lawn in front of his house. The only information reported about the possible killer was that someone had seen a black Range Rover in the area minutes before the murder took place. A little old lady who spent most of her time sitting by her window took notice of the Range Rover that was parked down the street from the house. She also reported to the police that she had seen an Hispanic looking man wearing a blue bandana around his head and sunglasses come out of the car.

The lady didn't pay too much attention to the Range Rover other than its color. However, she focused her attention on my convertible Volvo and she described me to the police perfectly. She told them my height, guesstimate my weight, what I was wearing, what time I got there, when I left and my plate number. She also mentioned that the guy in the Range Rover didn't come out of his car until after I left Phil's house. That old lady was like a neighborhood watchdog. I was now implicated in a murder that I had nothing to do with. She should have written down the license plate number of the Range Rover, I thought.

My license plate number, make and model of my car were blasted across every television screen for the public to see and the police department asked anyone with information about me to call their precinct immediately. I realized that I had been set up to take the fall for somebody else's crime. Why did that old woman have to live right across from Phil's house? The only thing the woman did that could've possibly saved my ass was the fact that she mentioned to the police that I didn't have any blood on my clothes and body when I left the house. She also told them that I didn't stay there very long. It didn't take a genius to know that I couldn't beat a man to death within minutes no matter what kind of weapon that was used.

I was in big trouble and my world was about to take a tumble that I was not prepared to deal with. My entire life, I had created an image that I was ashamed to expose to my family. I acted like a proper lady at home, but I was really a devilish whore who slept around with a bunch of men for no reason at all. And now they were about to discover the true me and I didn't know if they would reject me. I even worried about Darren finding out that I was sleeping around with so many men. I felt like a whore for the first time in my life. There was no rhyme or reason for my behavior other than my dependency on dicks.

I had to decide what I was going to do and how I was going to do it. It was a matter of time before the police showed up at my parents' doorstep to arrest me. I still hadn't change the address on my registration and license after I moved. The police wouldn't know how to find me at home because all my mail still went to my parents' house. And I damn sure didn't want the police to talk to my parents before I did.

Time was running out and I made the decision to pick up the phone to call my mom to tell her what was going on in my life. After explaining the whole situation to my mom, she assured me that everything was going to be all right. She called the family attorney and asked him to go down to the police station with me. My mom told me to drive straight to her house and that she would explain my ordeal to my dad. By the time I arrived at my parents' house, the police and my attorney were already there. I was under suspicion immediately because my family retained an attorney. We went down to the police station and I explained the situation to this handsome detective who was leading the case. My statement was recorded and I tried as much as I could to recall every little detail.

The police told me they were going to go to court to get a warrant to search my place and everything in my life just seemed very crazy and out of control to me at that point. My lawyer tried his best to explain the severity of my situation, but all I could think about was what Darren's reaction would be when he found out about Phil and all the other men that I had slept with. I also kept the fact that Phil had a run-in with Vinny from the police. Phil was all that Darren and the police needed to know about at that point.

Chapter 37

The police didn't have any evidence to charge me with anything, so I was able to go back home with my parents. The lawyer told me that until the cops had concrete evidence that I had anything to do with Phil's death; I really didn't have anything to worry about. He also asked me over and over if I was sure that I didn't have anything to do with Phil's murder. Even my own lawyer was questioning my innocence. I kept repeating to him that I had absolutely nothing to do with Phil's death because I really liked Phil in a sort of weird way. I had to tell him everything about the affair that I had with Phil. My parents never doubted my innocence from the time that I told them that I had nothing to do with the murder. However, the fact that I kept my relationship with Phil from them, surely raised their suspicion. My dad asked me if I was the reason why Phil left the company. I had to be honest with him, so I told him "yes". He just shook his head at me with disgust.

My parents insisted that I stayed at their house for safety, but I wanted to be by myself. I was too ashamed of myself because I knew that a lot was going to be revealed about me in the media when the cops were done with their investigation and none of it would paint a positive picture of me. I left my parents' house and drove straight home with my mother following behind me. My mother insisted on staying with me because she didn't want me to be alone at my house. She packed my father's nine millimeter handgun in her purse with an overnight bag. My dad was busy calling a few people of his own to get to the bottom of Phil's murder. He wanted to find out how and why I was implicated in something so tragic and serious.

When I pulled up to my driveway, I could see some of my neighbors looking at me through their window shades and curtains, rolling their eyes. To them, I was already guilty because my name was in the news and the police were looking for me. The fact that I was the only Black person living on that street didn't work at all in my favor. To top it off, I was never friendly to any of my neighbors because I knew they didn't want me to live on that street. They tried to get a petition signed to keep the previous owner from selling the house to me when I was trying to buy it. These people weren't my friends from the time I moved into the neighborhood and I didn't expect them to be my friends after this incident came to light.

After we both pulled into my two-car garage, my mother got out of her car and walked down to the end of the driveway and stuck her middle fingers out to all the neighbors who were looking through their shades and curtains. I knew none of them wanted to mess with a middle-aged Black woman who was packing a loaded nine millimeter. My mother had been there before. When she and my dad bought their house in Long Island back in the early eighties, their neighbors thought they could run them out. My father had never been the type of person to run from situations and my tiny little mother is even tougher than he is. They stayed and fought their neighbors' every mean attempt to force them to move. My father even joined a gun club and he let everyone on his street know that if they ever crossed the line with him, he wouldn't hesitate to bust a cap in their asses to protect his family.

I can never understand why white people in certain neighborhoods think they can dictate who can live in the neighborhood. They want to claim land that they stole from the Indians. They act like they should be the only ones privileged enough to live wherever the fuck they please. They're so sensitized by what they see on television about other minority races all the time, they don't even realize that some of us have just as much money as they do and sometimes even more. My parents never took the Martin Luther King approach when it came to protecting their family. It was always an eye for an eye and they taught me to always fight for what I want and that I should never let people push me around.

After my mother gave the fingers to the whole block, then bent down to point her ass up to tell them to kiss it, we walked inside my house and I noticed that my answering machine light was blinking and it had seven messages posted. I pressed the button to listen to the messages. The first three messages were from Darren. He was worried because he had seen the news footage. The other four were from my cowardice neighbors telling me that they didn't want a murderer living on their street. Of course, every single one of them had their phone numbers blocked. I was really happy that my mother was with me because I needed her support and comfort.

I was trying to figure out what I was going to say to Darren, but I couldn't think of the right words. He knew that I had been out with other men, but he never expected me to be fucking them. Although he never admitted to sleeping with any of the women that he hung out with, I knew that Darren was no saint and he couldn't fool me even if he tried. I was about to get caught in my game and there was no way out. All that innocent bullshit role that I had been playing up to now, Darren accepted. Would he react differently if I told him that Phil was one of my lovers? I wondered. Phil wasn't just any lover; he was the only other man that I cared for besides Darren.

My mother could sense that I had something on my mind. She asked me if I wanted to talk about it over a hot cup of cocoa. She went to the kitchen to heat up some water to make us some hot cocoa. My mother has known that I like a lot of milk in my hot cocoa since I was a little girl, so when she returned with two cups of hot cocoa in hand, she informed me that she had put plenty of milk in mine. I just smiled at her because she was still trying to be my mother. My mother knew just what to do to make me comfortable enough to open up to her too. Honestly, I really needed to talk to someone that I could trust.

As my mother and I sat in the family room sipping on cocoa, I started divulging to her my personal business from the time I was in college. I told her that I had been addicted to sex since I was a teenager, but I didn't start having sex until I got to college. I'm no fool- some things have to remain sacred no matter how cool you think a parent might be. There was no way in the world that I was gonna tell my mother that I had been sucking dicks since high school. We were cool, but she was still my mother. I didn't know what to expect from my mother after I told her that I enjoyed sex more than the average person and that I was into variety. My mom simply pulled me towards her to give me a big hug and told me that there was nothing wrong with me and that sex was natural.

My perception of the way my mother viewed me changed completely. She was very accepting and supportive. I started telling her about Vinny and the incident that took place with him and Phil. My mother became very suspicious of Vinny and told me that I had to tell the police about him. She was ninety nine percent sure that Vinny probably had something to do with Phil's death.

When I told her my reasons for not telling the police about Vinny, she put it simply to me, "Tina, in life, sometimes we have to make decisions that's gonna change the way people feel about us. It could be positive or negative, but most of the time the change is usually negative and sometimes we are afraid of that negative reaction. If you think that Darren would want nothing to do with you because you slept with a few other men while you guys were apart, then he's not the man for you. Risking your freedom because you're withholding information from the police for a man that you're not certain about is not worth it. The only people whose reaction you should be worried about is your family. And you should know that your daddy and I love you too much to ever hate anything about you. When we brought you into this world, we weren't perfect and we don't expect you to be perfect either. I can tell you one thing, though. I'm not ready to see my daughter go to jail for a crime she did not commit".

After listening to my mother, I knew that I was going to tell Darren the truth and I didn't give a damn how he took it. If Darren cared about me as much as he claimed, what I did when we were apart should not matter to him. Besides, it was always his idea for us to spend time apart. I didn't expect Darren to love me unconditionally, but there were certain conditions that I was not willing to put up with and being the perfect little angel was one of them. As much as Darren and I had sex, he should've had at least, an idea that I loved sex and I had to fulfill my sexual needs when we weren't together. It's not like we were totally committed to each other when I slept with these men. I'm crazy about Darren, but I'm not willing to lose myself because of him.

After my mother and I finished our little conversation, we went upstairs to clean up before bed. She used the guest bathroom to shower and I showered in my own private bathroom. My dad called to make sure that everything was okay with us. He also told me not to worry about anything because he had his people working on it as well. My dad also told me that he loved me before he got off the phone and I couldn't resist telling him how much I adored and loved him. My mother and I stayed up late that night to watch a repeat of Waiting to Exhale on UPN, The Negro Network. In between commercials, I told my mother about the many letters that I found in Phil's closet and we started to wonder if perhaps he was killed by one of those women. After the movie, my mother went to sleep in my bed with me the same way she did when I was a scared little girl.

Chapter 38

I didn't even bother returning Darren's calls. I wanted to have a goodnight sleep without having to deal with more problems from Darren. I woke up the next day feeling rejuvenated and I wrote a to-do list. One of the first things that I wanted to do was to place a call to that handsome detective in charge of the case. I believed his name was Romeo Williams. My mother was an early bird even on the weekends. She had beaten me to the kitchen to make breakfast. After inhaling the aroma of fresh strawberry flavored pancakes made from scratch and scrambled eggs coming from the kitchen, I knew that I was in for a treat. I went back upstairs to brush my teeth.

When I returned downstairs, my mother and I sat at the kitchen table and we ate our breakfast like two best friends who were spending valuable time with each other. After breakfast, we went to our separate bathrooms to take a shower. I had called the police station to leave a message for detective Williams telling him to expect me in his office around eleven o'clock that morning. I wore a nice pair of tight fitted Jeans with a v-neck sweater and my leather jacket.

My mother rode with me to the police station where we met with our lawyer and the detective. I told detective Williams about Vinny and how he had been stalking me for months. I also told him about the two run-ins he had with Phil. When detective Williams asked me why I withheld that piece information about Vinny from him in the beginning, I told him I was scared and it was something more personal than anything. Detective Williams was trying to interrogate me, but my lawyer would have none of it. We cut the meeting short then left the police station.

I went back home that day thinking about how everyone thought I was responsible for something that I had nothing to do with and how it was going to possibly ruin my personal life. I even stopped thinking that detective Williams was handsome after he tried to interrogate me. I needed to straighten things out with Darren and the longer I waited the worst things were going to be. I told my mother that I was going to be all right and that she could go back home to take care of her business. I literally had to push the lady out of my house because she wouldn't leave me alone. My mother was trying to treat me like a little girl and I had enough of it already. I was a grown ass woman who got myself into the trouble that I was in and I needed to find a way to get out of it. I love my mother for being supportive, but I was getting tired of the smothering.

After my mother left, I picked up the phone to call Darren to tell him what was going on with me. I didn't even get a chance to finish telling him about Phil before he started blowing his top. Darren was trying to make me feel guilty about sleeping with Phil and he hadn't even heard about Vinny and all the other men. I put the phone down on the bed while he went on a tantrum. When I came back to the phone, I asked him if he was done and he calmly told me "yeah". All I said was "okay, there's more". He started going off again without even hearing what the rest of the stuff I was going to tell him was about. I was only trying to tell him the parts that he didn't hear on the news. After I mentioned that I slept with Vinny on the night that I went to meet him at the after-work spot, he called me a "ho" then hung up the phone.

I had never seen that immature side of Darren and I didn't want to see anymore of it. If he was mad then, he was going to be even angrier later when the rest of the story came out. Darren had the opportunity to hear everything straight from my mouth, but his anger clouded his ability to think rationally and he was going to get the bad version of me that was going to be exposed on the evening news.

Chapter 39

A few weeks had gone by before I received a call from the police precinct's Captain Washington, informing me that detective Williams had been removed from the case. My lawyer had a special meeting with the police department and he determined that Mr. Williams' bias views of me took away the objectivity of the case. Mr. Williams was adamant that I was involved in Phil's murder and he swore that I was trying to fool everybody into thinking that I was innocent. He never even followed up on the information about the Range Rover that he received from the old lady who lived across the street from Phil. His total focus was on me and only me. My daddy had hired a private investigator to tag Mr. Williams and he was the one who informed my daddy that Mr. Williams was following me around everyday. My daddy immediately called our lawyer to have Mr. Williams removed from the case.

My lawyer didn't have Mr. Williams remove from the case just because he focused the attention of the case on me. He had him removed because my daddy was worried about my well-being. My mother had told him about my situation with Vinny and my daddy took the fact that Vinny was still walking around a free man, seriously. He wanted to make sure that I wasn't going to be Vinny's next victim. In addition, my father hired private security guards to look after me twenty fours without my knowledge.

During my conversation with Captain Washington, he also informed me about the new detective on the case, her name was Tracey Childs and she would be in contact with me very soon. I heard the part about Mr. Williams' behavior from my father after he was informed by the lawyer. I couldn't understand why this man had it in for me. I was trying to figure out if I might've slept with him in the past and didn't remember him for some reason, but I couldn't recall anything about him. He was a little too old for me to have been with him, anyway.

Meanwhile, the private investigator was gathering more information on Vinny than the police department ever could. He was able to find out that Vinny also had a loft downtown Manhattan where he spent his weekdays that he never told me about. There, he was using a black Range Rover of a friend who went out of town and left his keys with Vinny so he could move his car to the alternate sides of the street every-day for street cleaning. Vinny must've figured that he could use his friend's car to follow me to go kill Phil and no one would ever know it was him.

Vinny had everything planned, but the investigator caught a lot of lucky breaks. He was there when Vinny's friend returned to pick up his car keys from him and he took pic-tures of them in case the police didn't believe him. Vinny had tried to disguise himself as an Hispanic gang member when he followed me from my job to Phil's house on the day of the murder. Since I had no knowledge of this Range Rover and I was busy looking for a black Porsche on my rearview mirror, it was easy for him to follow me. I didn't even pay attention to the truck. The fact that he was wearing a bandana and sun-glasses to disguise himself as Hispanic probably threw me off as well. Vinny could easily pass himself as Hispanic because of his dark olive complexion. He was just too bright a man to be that crazy.

Vinny must've thought he was a real Italian gangster because he waited for a few days before he threw away in the Hudson River, the clothes that he was wearing when he beat Phil to death with the bat. By then, the private investigator had been following him and watching his every move. It was easy for the investigator to retrieve the plastic bag with the bloody clothes, the bat and the shoes that Vinny wore when he killed Phil. The private investigator had all the evidence that he needed to hand over to the police so they could arrest and charge Vinny with first degree murder.

A meeting was set between the police department, my father, my lawyer and the private investigator. They felt like it was an open and shut case, but the police department saw it another way. Even though they found the murder weapon, clothes and enough evidence to determine that Vinny was the killer, it would still be the private investigator's words against Vinny's. Yes, the blood on the bat matched Phil's blood and the clothes found were covered with Phil's blood, but that didn't mean anything to the police because there wasn't a shred of evidence that the clothes belonged to Vinny and the station's forensic scientist couldn't even find his prints on anything that was brought to the station. Vinny was a step ahead of everybody except the new lead investigator on the case.

Chapter 40

It took Tracey Childs almost fifteen years to make detective on the police force. She had to work twice as hard as the male officers to earn her stripes and she was fed up with the idea that she couldn't cut it as detective because she was female. While all the male officers had their heads up their asses, Tracey was busy looking for clues to close the case. When I first met Tracey, I could instantly tell that she wasn't into men and the idea of having a man bang away at her pussy would've been repulsive to her. Being around my lesbian ex-best friend for four years in college, I was able to pick up on a lot of stuff about lesbians. I was able to identify the masculine lesbians and the feminine ones. Tracey was a feminist all the way, which placed her more on the masculine side of the persuasion. Her body language was feminine but her demeanor was masculine.

She was very pretty and there was something about her eyes that made me curious about her. Tracey was probably in her late thirties, but she looked no older than twenty five. I only assumed that she was in her late thirties because of the length of time that she told me she had been on the force. She was about 5 ft 8inches tall with a toned build. Her weight had to be about one hundred and thirty pounds and she had a firm grip when she shook my hand. Tracey was the first woman that I had found attractive since college. I had never looked at another woman since that experience with my roommate, Tanya, back in college, but I found Tracey to be very sexy. Maybe it was because of her take-charge attitude.

Tracey's approach about the case was very different than detective Williams. She talked to me like a friend and she tried to learn as much as she could about my relationship with Phil. She wasn't gung ho about my innocence or guilt. She simply wanted to know the facts. Since I told her that Phil had knocked out Vinny in the past during a confrontation, she focused more on the fact that he probably fought for his life and that Vinny probably didn't walk away unscathed from the incident. She knew that Phil's street smarts would have allowed him to hurt Vinny at least a little during their physical scuffle.

Over the next few weeks, Tracey worked relentlessly to find the clues that would link Vinny to the case. She inconspicuously followed Vinny around and she looked for any kind of discomfort or pain coming from him. One day while he was sitting at a bar in Manhattan, he was bumped by a waitress on her way to bring drinks to a customer and his chest hit the counter. When he turned around to react with his fist and holding his chest because of the obvious pain from the bump, he was disappointed to see that it was a beautiful waitress who had bumped him. Tracey had gotten the clue she was looking for. Vinny was obviously hurt by Phil and Tracey wanted to find out the extent of his injuries.

Chapter 41

Meanwhile, my physical attraction to Tracey was getting stronger and stronger. I wasn't sure if it was because of her strong determination to solve the case, or the confidence that she displayed when she spoke, but I wanted to sleep with her. Of course, I did not act on my sexual urges, but I sure as hell masturbated enough in my room while I thought about Tracey's tongue between my legs and her slow hands caressing my whole body. I bought this sexual toy called "The Silver Bullet", which I used to stimulate my clit through motorized vibration and I couldn't get enough of it. I used that thing every night before I went to bed thinking about Tracey and I came every single time.

Since I wasn't getting any dick from Darren, I needed to satisfy my needs. Everything in my world may have been chaotic at the time, but that didn't mean that I didn't have needs. I even hooked up with Bobby, my old flame from college. I met him while I was at a club in Manhattan with one of my girlfriends. After I mentioned to her how this guy used to tear my pussy up back in college, she agreed to have a three-some with me and him. And true to his old self, Bobby fucked the hell out of both of us and my girlfriend became afraid of him. She swore to me that no one had ever hit her G-spot like Bobby did and she told me that she couldn't be around a man who could fuck like that all the time because she would lose her mind.

After my great night of fun and excitement with Bobby and my girlfriend, I sort of wanted to keep in touch with him in a way in case I ever went down to Maryland for a visit. Bobby told me that he had relocated to Silver Springs, Maryland after he graduated from college. He was in New York for a conference when I ran into him. I ended up spending the whole weekend with him at his hotel in Manhattan. Bobby fucked me just like old times and we enjoyed each other's company the way we did back in college. However, I could tell that Bobby wasn't as comfortable with me when he was leaving. I had to guess that he had a girlfriend back home waiting for him. We didn't talk about exchanging numbers. He just told me it was nice to run into each other again. Bobby had become a very successful computer engineer working for a well-known computer engineering firm in Maryland and he was as handsome as ever. He definitely got better-looking with age. It was just one for the road between me and Bobby.

Chapter 42

Tracey knew that time was crucial to her investigation. She didn't want to give Vinny enough time to heal from whatever wound that he received at the hands of Phil. One night while she was at another bar watching Vinny, she decided to throw herself at him. It was easy bait because Tracey was just too attractive for him to resist. He invited her to his house and before he knew it, she had him lying butt naked on his back across his bed with his hands tied to the headboard. After confirming that he had indeed been wounded by Phil with a hard punch to his chest that obviously broke a couple of his ribs because he was all blue in the chest, she went to the other room to use his phone to call her cell phone. After picking up the phone, she told him that she was disappointed that they couldn't continue their little charade because she had an emergency and had to leave immediately. She left him tied to his bedpost butt naked.

Tracey had done her job as an undercover police officer and it was time for her to get a warrant for Vinny's arrest. She ran back to her captain with the newly discovered evidence and a warrant was issued for Vinny's arrest. When the fact that Vinny had been arrested for the murder of Phil came to light in the media, it was unfortunately too late for me. All my sexual trysts with the many different men that I had slept with had been publicized through the course of the police department's investigation. My daddy would look at me differently and even my brother was surprised that his little sister had been with so many men.

I had brought shame to my family as far as they were concerned. The only person who stood by me at the time was my mother. She never once believed that I was a bad person and she tried her hardest to convince my daddy that half the stuff they were saying about me on television weren't true.

I was the only person who knew that the police investigators were telling the truth. The true characters of some of the men that I considered "cool" when I was in college started to come out. Kevin especially came out to slander my name in the media. He must've still been feeling hurt from me dumping him back in college. It's not like we were ever a couple or anything, but what could I do? There were others that took stabs at me for one reason or another and they were running their mouths like rats. I never in my life believed that men could talk so much. These men were worse than bitches.

A few weeks later, the media would have a better, much juicier story involving a white Wall Street big wig caught up in a love triangle. Even though much of the attention shifted to Vinny, I was still part of the story. The fact that Vinny had used his friend's Range Rover to drive to Phil's house to commit the crime had come to light weeks later and the forensic scientists were able to determine that the injuries that Vinny received at the hand of Phil during their scuffle, were consistent with the bruises found on Phil's knuckles at the time of his death.

Tracey was able to establish that Vinny had gotten into Phil's house through the back entrance. He wore white latex gloves and thermal underclothes to avoid leaving any traces of himself at the crime scene. Vinny timed the whole thing perfectly, but the old lady who lived across the street gave the private investigator and Tracey all the clues that they needed to bust him. Even though Vinny's dumb ass had washed his thermal underclothes, the police department's forensic scientist was still able to detect a little bit of blood that probably seeped through his shirt after a search of his house. And it was determined by the lab that the blood found on Vinny's clothes belong to Phil.

When Vinny's lawyers figured out that they were cornered, they offer to take a plea from the prosecutor. However, it was a little too late because they had nothing to bargain with. The case went to trial a year later and Vinny was found guilty of first degree murder by a jury of his peers. I was relieved to learn that Vinny was finally going to spend the rest of his life behind bars. It took a little while, but I was able to let go of my paranoia.

Chapter 43

During the entire time while I was going through my trials and tribulations of being implicated and vindicated for a murder, I never once heard from Darren. I don't know if it was because I hurt him so badly or maybe because he thought that I was a whore that he needed to wash his hands off me, but I still missed him. I ran into the arms of Tracey for comfort and she provided a lot more than I expected. During the investigation, Tracey kept her distance from me, but I later found out that she could sense that I was attracted to her from the first time we met. As a professional, she couldn't get involved with a suspect because it would completely take away the objectivity of the case. For some reason, she knew that I would still be around after the case was over. Tracey must've believed in my innocence from the very beginning.

She and I went out on our first date on the day that Vinny was found guilty of murder. I got to know Tracey a little better and I found out she was abandoned by her parents as a young girl and she grew up in the foster care system in New York City. There, she was transferred from home to home and was molested and raped by many different men. She left the system when she turned eighteen. She was able to attend John Jay University where she received a degree in criminal justice. After graduating from college, Tracey joined the Suffolk County Police Department and she had hoped to transfer to the Special Victims Unit one day.

Tracey also told me that she could tell that I was digging her from the time we met. I asked her what she thought of me as a person with all that shit she was hearing in the media. She told me that she never looked to the media to form an opinion of someone. However, she didn't think I was capable to committing murder. According to the media, Tracey should have never made it this far in life and she never took any thing that was reported to heart until after she heard all the facts. I liked the fact that she had an open mind right away.

I'd been having a great time with Tracey, but the one thing I wanted in life, she could never give me. I have always wanted to have a normal family consisting of my husband and children. Tracey was a good partner and a friend and we had so much in common, but I had always wanted a husband and the only person I ever thought could be my husband was Darren. I talked to Tracey a lot about him and she knew how much I cared for Darren. Sometimes, I could tell that Tracey only sat there and listened to me ramble on about Darren because she cared about me, but I knew that she wished that she could magically find a way to get me pregnant. I loved Tracey and if I was a full blown lesbian, she would have been my chosen partner, but I was not a lesbian. I wasn't even bisexual. I later found out that I was just experimenting.

It was hard enough on my dad when he heard that I had been sleeping with so many men, I didn't think he could handle the fact that I was also licking pussies and sucking on tits, in addition. Tracey always had a problem with me because I wanted to keep our relationship a secret from my parents and private from the public. Whenever she tried to force me to hold her hand out in public, we always ended up in an argument or a fight. Tracey was comfortable with her sexuality and the fact that she loved women. I was still enjoying sex and discovering myself. But the one thing I liked about us was the make-up sex after a fight.

I remember one day I got into this big argument with Tracey because I handed my number to a guy that I knew when I was a kid that I ran into while I was with her. This chick tried to scold me like I was a little kid and I went ballistic on her. I told her "I ain't your little fucking daughter that you can boss around and scream at whenever you want. I'm a grown ass woman and I will do with myself and my pussy whatever I want, when I want to and how I want to". Tracey

146

had never seen that side of me and she was shocked when it finally came out. I caught the train back home that day and left her stranded by herself in Manhattan.

The next day, she showed up at my house with a dozen roses and a card in hand to apologize. She also wore a nice pair of red pumps, a teddy under her trench coat, with nothing else. She smelled very fresh and clean and my nipples were hard at the sight of her. I knew that I was also sorry for going off on her, so I didn't even give her time to utter the words "I'm sorry" before we locked lips. I kissed her sensually on the lips for about thirty seconds until she opened her mouth and invited my tongue to wrap around hers in a French kiss that was so passionate, I didn't even remember when we made it upstairs to my bedroom rolling around on top of each other on my king size bed.

Tracey positioned my back up against the headboard while she impetuously sucked on my breasts until I became wetter than a baby's bib. She licked around my breasts and my nipples while rubbing my clit with her fingers. The sensual touch of her hands had an affect on me and it was always hard to contain myself. I slid down on the satin sheets to lie down on my back, Tracey got on top of me and she started rubbing her pussy against mine while she stuck her tongue in and out of my mouth. By the time I sat Tracey up to lick her pussy, she had already reached into my drawer to grab my Silver Bullets. I took one from her and I started rubbing it against her clit until she climaxed and shook out of control in my arms.

After Tracey came, she went down on me with the Silver Bullet in hand. She ate me while sticking the tip of the Silver Bullet inside of me until I let out a loud roar like lioness who was about to come in the hot jungles of Africa. I came multiple times while Tracey ate me and afterwards, we just laid in bed holding each other like there were never any disagreements or arguments to begin with.

Chapter 44

Loving only Tracey for almost a year was really hard for me. I struggled with monogamy and I didn't know how much longer I was going to stay monogamous to Tracey. I was still missing Darren even after all this time. I didn't mind being with Tracey, but I really needed Darren. I started to believe that monogamy was not for everybody. It certainly wasn't for me because I had gotten use to having a variety of people to please me. Though I didn't want the number of partners that I had to be as high as they were, there was nothing I could do about it. I wanted to find Darren. No, I needed to find Darren. Being penetrated with a strap-on dildo did not satisfy me like a real penis did.

I knew that running into Darren wouldn't be so hard. I knew that he had never stopped going to that after-work spot even after we decided to become exclusive with each other. It was the one place that I knew I could casually run into him and I could react based on his actions. I needed a breather from Tracey because we had been spending almost every moment together. So, I told her that I was gonna go out the upcoming Thursday to spend a little time by myself. Tracey had made it a habit of spending about three nights a week at my house and I felt like she was suffocating me. I told her that I would be home late that evening and that she should probably go home and not wait up for me.

It had been so long since I had seen Darren even my parents stopped asking me questions about him. But I still couldn't get him out of my mind. I couldn't wait for Thursday to arrive so I could finally go down to Manhattan at Cheetah's to accidentally run into him. I went through my closet looking for some of the sexiest outfits I could find. After I took out about ten different outfits and lay them down on the bed, the process of elimination began. I stood in front of my mirror on Wednesday evening to try on every single one of the outfits before Tracey came to my house. One by one I found reasons why this one or that one didn't look so good on me. I really couldn't ask Tracey for her opinion because her nosey ass would have wanted to know why I was trying to look so sexy. Then finally, I picked up this little black dress with spaghetti straps that complemented my every asset. I always had a flat stomach, so I never had to worry about any bulges when I wore my tight fitted dresses. This little black dress was tight and sleek and it sat on my ass and held up my large breasts in a way that even a blind man could see them.

That night when Tracey came to my house, I had sex with her while I was thinking about Darren the whole time. I just wanted a moment with Darren. I went right to sleep afterwards and I didn't even bother to allow Tracey to hold me in her arms like she usually did while we slept. On Thursday morning, I woke up feeling very happy anticipating a reconnection with Darren. After Tracey made her way out the door, I started singing this little song that I made up for Darren "I'm going to see my man again today and it's gonna be a good day". I was just being silly that morning and even when I got to work that morning, my mother could see the excitement on my face. I didn't want to tell her about my plans in case Darren rejected my efforts.

It seemed like the day was longer for some reason and it went by very slowly. I left work at four thirty that afternoon and I drove frantically to my house. I couldn't wait to take a nice shower, shave my legs, my underarms and panty line. I wanted to be all fresh and clean when I saw Darren. I rubbed this strawberry scented lotion from Victoria's Secret all over my body because I knew it was Darren's favorite. I also wore his favorite perfume, Forever, which I had stopped wearing because it was old. I didn't even like that perfume to begin with, but I wore it to please Darren. My hair was looking bouncy and shiny and my make-up was flawless. I was looking and feeling good. I left my house feeling confident that Darren was going to be in my life again.

I made it to the Midtown tunnel in no time. By the time I pulled up in the parking lot near the place, I could see the line forming at Cheetah's. I strolled towards the back of the line and I could see that all the men were staring while the women rolled their eyes hating on my banging ass dress. Even the guy at the front door noticed me right away and he told me that a beautiful woman like myself should never have to wait in the back of anybody's line as he ushered me to the front. My confidence was at an all time high. I playfully gave the guy at the front door a kiss on the cheek and thanked him as I made my way into the lounge. Now that I was inside, the game was on.

Cheetah's was crowded but it was not packed. I positioned myself at the bar so that I could be seen by anybody who walked through the door. I had already made my round inside the club to look for Darren and I couldn't find him anywhere. Since I couldn't find him, I was gonna let him find me. I had a surprise for Darren as well. I had changed my hairstyle since he last saw me. When I was with him, I wore my hair long with bangs in the front. I had decided to cut my hair short to that new style Halle Berry was rocking when she won her Oscar. I sat at the bar with a drink in my hand facing the front door. I was down to my third drink when Darren finally walked through the door wearing a black single breasted suit with flat front pants, a yellow and white striped shirt and a solid yellow tie to match. He also wore black shoes and a black belt. Darren had become more edgy as a dresser, but he looked good. His physique appeared to have been intact as I noticed his bulging biceps when he raised his hand to fix the knot on his tie.

It seemed like Darren was coming right at me as he fixed his tie around his neck. I quickly spun myself around to give him a view of my backside and silky smooth shoulders. After about thirty seconds of waiting for Darren to come up and whisper something in my ear, I turned around to find him hugging a woman standing a few feet from me. Disappointment is not a strong enough word to describe the way I felt, but I was not going to give up without a fighting chance. While he hugged the woman he had his back to me and I could see the woman's face over his right shoulder. She was an attractive woman, but she was no match for me. She didn't have enough T&A (tits and ass) to knock me out of the competition. She was even smiling as she glanced over to me while hugging my man. I didn't even pay her any mind.

I wanted to wait for the right opportunity to get up from my seat to walk to the other side of the lounge. I knew that my dress was irresistible and I knew from the moment that Darren laid eyes on my curvaceous body he'd want to know who I was. After ordering a couple of drinks, for himself and his friend, Darren turned around to get a view of the crowd in the club and I knew it was the opportunity that I was looking for. I got up strutting my ass across the floor like I was Tyra Banks in the middle of a Victoria's Secret lingerie fashion show. I could hear his girlfriend telling him to stop staring at my ass and I couldn't help but notice all the rest of the men staring at me also. I knew if he was the Darren of old he would find a way to get at me in the club. I knew that Darren had no idea it was me because of my new hairstyle, but there are some things about a man that can never change. Darren was always a sucker for women with nice asses and sexy walks and I knew I had both.

I walked to the other side and found a seat in the lounge not too far from the dance floor. Many men approached me for a dance and I turned every single one of them down. I was waiting for Darren because he was the reason why I got all dolled up to come to this place. I didn't really care too much about the place because it brought back too many bad memories. I sat and waited and waited and Darren never showed. I was losing my patience, so I walked back to the bar about an hour later to go find him and there was no sign of Darren. Just as I was about to walk towards the front of the place to get some fresh air, I noticed Darren leaving hand in hand with his new girlfriend. They were kissing all over each other and smiling happy like they were in love. Darren had changed. He was no longer what I thought of him. Perhaps, he had grown for the better as a man.

I disappointedly left the club that night and went home to sob. It was still early when I got home, so I stayed up to watch Jay Leno and eat about half a pint of ice cream before I went to bed. That night, I got no sleep at all. I tossed and turned on the bed until sun up and I woke up feeling very tired the next morning. I went to work with big bags under my eyes and my mother wondered why I looked so bad. I wanted to tell her so badly what I did the night before, but I chose not to because I didn't want to hear it from her.

Chapter 45

A couple more months had gone by and I resigned with the fact that I had lost Darren forever. Tracey was also starting to get on my nerves. She was always complaining about something. Sometimes, the relationship was just too catty for me. I started to believe that I was not a lesbian at all. I was drawn to Tracey because she was there for me in my times of need. I'm not talking about emotional needs because my mother had been there emotionally every step of the way. I'm talking about sexual and physical needs. I needed someone to hold, touch and please me and Tracey fulfilled those needs. But she had really been working my last nerves. I didn't keep it a secret that I missed Darren and the thrusting of his penis inside of me from Tracey and she had been trying her hardest to prove to me that a man's dick was not as satisfying as woman's tongue. That tongue had been licking me for quite some time now and I still wanted to have a nice meaty dick inside of me. Not to mention the fact that Darren ate me better than any lesbian ever could.

Tracey started to remind me of Vinny in a way. She was trying to compete with someone that was not on the same level as her as far as my heart was concerned. And furthermore, she could never provide the one thing that I wanted in my future, which was a child. She thought just because she could strap on a dildo she was equal to a man. I had to explain to that her that a dildo is not a dick no matter how big and long it is. Don't get me wrong, I used a dildo to masturbate all the time, but that's just for instant gratification. Bottom line, I needed a dick because I also wanted to have a family. Sure, I would adopt, but not until after I tried to have at least one biological child of my own. And that's one of the things that I like about Tracey also, she wanted to open her heart to help disadvantaged children. She had wanted to adopt a couple of kids since she became a police officer, but she didn't want to do it alone.

She wanted me to be part of her plans, but I wanted to try to have at least one with my husband, not my lover. As great a person as Tracey could be sometimes, she was also a pain in the ass when she didn't get what she wanted. She and I would be bumping heads too much if we stayed together and I would never be totally satisfied. Honestly, I'd had enough of this lesbian shit and I was ready to go back to my dicks. I told Tracey she would always have my help when she decided to adopt those children.

Tracey was at least trying to do more than a lot of those rich Black people in Hollywood. I'm tired of black folks whining and crying about the fact that people like Tom Cruise, Steven Spielberg and other White people are adopting black children. Instead of complaining, why don't they do the same? It's easy to say that a Black child would do better in a Black home, but how many of those homes are coming to their rescue? Sometimes, we're the biggest hypocrites and we do nothing but run our mouths for the sake of running it. I applaud those white people who choose to adopt black children and offer them a better life. If you really think about it, the alternative is the Foster Care system or the streets. Black people need to put up or shut up, especially those in Hollywood who think that owning fifty cars and a fifty room mansion that they can show on MTV Crib is part of a lifestyle.

Perhaps, Tracey was more apt to these children's conditions because she went through the system and understood their needs, but it doesn't take a genius to know that we have many poor children in this country that are in need. I look forward to the day when I can open my door to a child in need. Even my own parents were too selfish to open their door to a child in need. Tracey has taught me a lot and I'm glad that she came into my life, but I'm still not a lesbian and I'm no longer curious.

Chapter 46

On a Saturday afternoon when I took my car to the local car wash to get it clean after the meltdown of a big snow storm, I ran into Darren. He pulled up behind me in the line to get his car washed as well. He must've been doing a lot better because he had traded in his old car for a brand new Mercedes S class. I didn't even know it was him until I got out of my car to let the people at the car wash vacuum the interior. Actually, he was the one who noticed me.

Surprisingly, Darren walked up to me and asked if I was still mad at him. I didn't know what the hell he was talking about, so I asked him "What do you mean? I thought you were the one who was mad at me?" I thought he was trying to pull a reversal role on me when he told me "Look, Tina, you don't have to pretend that you don't hate me. I know that I acted like a jerk when you came clean to me, but you could've at least answered my calls". I was thinking to myself "what calls!" This fool was standing in front of me telling me that he had been calling me, but somehow I never received his messages.

I was giving Darren the cold shoulder and he started losing his patience with me. "Look, I don't want to argue. I just wanted to tell you in person that I'm sorry and I wished things could be different. Also, I missed you very much. The number is still the same if you ever want to talk to me again", he said. Darren had never sounded so sincere to me in his life. I had been yearning for this man and here he was apologizing and asking for my forgiveness. I shrugged off his apology and I said to him "it was nice seeing you too, but I have to go. Take care of yourself".

When the guy pulled up with my car in the front after wiping it down, my heart was beating a mile a minute. I was so excited to see Darren I didn't know how to contain myself. I hopped in my car and felt giddy inside. I drove straight to the Roosevelt Field Mall to buy some lingerie. Darren had made me feel so sexy that day I wanted to wear something special to bed that evening even if I wasn't going to be with him.

When I got home that evening, I was still happy from my run-in with Darren. I went to the dining room to my wine rack and I opened a bottle of bubbly. I poured a glass of white wine then went upstairs to take a long bath. When I got upstairs I couldn't help but notice that Tracey had left her purse by the bed with her wallet in it. She must've forgotten the bag by accident. It was normal for Tracey to leave a few items at my house while we were dating. Most of the items were lingerie or clothes that she wore to work. But when I saw her purse on the floor by the bed, I decided to take a peek inside. I really don't have a reason for why I did it, but I wanted to do it.

As I went through the items in her purse one by one, I didn't notice anything that was out of the ordinary. She had a few things in there like lip gloss, mascara, lipstick and other feminine items that she might need in case her friend Little Red Riding hood came for a surprise visit for the month. However, there was one compartment in her purse where she kept a mini cassette tape that was the same brand that I kept on my answering machine. Since the Maxwell brand was very popular, I didn't think much of the tape, at first. I placed everything back in her purse and then I went in the bathroom to run the water in the tub for a nice bath. After the tub was filled with water and my favorite strawberry scented bubble bath foam, I laid in the tub for almost an hour playing with myself and sipping wine. I even allowed the water pressure from the faucet to hit my clit until I reached an orgasm or two.

After my long bath, I walked out of the tub and the purse was still in the corner staring at me. I didn't really want to invade Tracey's privacy by snooping through her personal belongings, but something about the tape kept drawing my curiosity. I thought about the possibility of the tape being someone's confession that she forgot to turn in to the police station. I didn't want to implicate myself in some murder mystery that Tracey was trying to solve, but my curiosity got the best of me. I took the tape out of her purse and I brought it downstairs and popped it in my answering machine to listen to it. I was shocked to hear Darren's voice on the tape leaving me many messages pleading to see me and to give our relationship another chance. He must've left about ten messages, overall. And with each one he was begging more for forgiveness and telling me that he wanted to be there for me during my times of trials and apologizing to me. At first, I was angry, I couldn't believe that Tracey had betrayed me like that. I wanted to throw all her shit out of my house. She purposely sabotaged my relationship with Darren for her own benefit.

I never suspected that Tracey could do something like that. She must've switched the tapes when she suggested that my outgoing message was too boring and that I needed a new one. I allowed her to record my new outgoing message without thinking much of it and that must've been the time when she switched the tapes. That conniving bitch was the reason why I never got back with Darren. She tried as much as she could to say negative things about Darren and I was so angry with him, I allowed it. She kept telling me about how he deserted me when I was most in need and she called him a selfish egotistical asshole who only had his best interest at heart.

I always stood up for Darren because I knew he wasn't that kind of man, but she kept drilling in my head that he was never good for me. Now, I saw where all that shit was leading. Tracey must've thought she was real smart trying to get me to hate Darren. It was time to use one of her own tricks against her. I took the tape with her outgoing message out of the answering machine and placed it in her purse. I took the other one with Darren's messages and placed it in my answering machine.

I knew that Tracey wouldn't know that I switched the tapes back because she always called me on my cell phone to reach me. I don't ever recall her calling me on my home phone. Darren wasn't able to call me on my cell phone because I had changed my number when he and I stopped talking. That was one of the reasons why I never spoke with him. It was also her suggestion for me to get a new phone. I couldn't wait to see the look on Tracey's face after she was busted.

Chapter 47

While I was in the living room chilling on my couch watching some boring movie on Lifetime, Tracey called to ask me to meet her at this little posh restaurant in Long Island. I acted like I was excited to meet with her when I was on the phone. She had no idea that it was going to be the last time that we ever did anything together as a couple. I wore one of my sexy dresses because Tracey always loved me in a dress. She was the pants suit type. I showed up at the restaurant at eight o'clock as scheduled. On my way to the restaurant, I called my home phone to reactivate the messages that Darren left so that the little red light would be blinking on the answering machine when I walked in the house later with Tracey.

I tried to act as normal as I could with Tracey at the restaurant. She kept flirting with me under the table and telling me how she couldn't wait to get home to lick every inch of my body. Under normal circumstances, I would've gotten wet when she reached across under the table to rub her big toe against my clit, but I was in no mood to be toe fucked. I simply smiled at her. I couldn't wait to get home so I could put this bitch in her place. She thought she could play me like I was a dumb little girl.

After dinner, she suggested that we go for a walk down by the park. I declined and told her it was too cold for me to be outside walking. I told her I wanted to go home because there were a few things that I wanted to show her. Of course, in her mind she thought it was something sexual, but I couldn't wait to see the look on her face when she found out the real reason that I wanted to go home. She followed me to my house and after we pulled up in the garage I didn't closed the door behind me. I left the garage door up and I opened the door leading to the kitchen to get in. Tracey told me that I forgot to close the garage door, and I told her not to worry about it that I'd close it in a few minutes. Tracey went to the living room while I went to the kitchen to get a glass of water. I needed to be calm before I confronted her conniving ass.

Since Darren hadn't called me in a few months, she never expected to hear his voice on my answering machine ever again. She thought she had gotten rid of him for good. While I was in the kitchen, I asked her if there were any messages on the answering machine. She looked over to the answering machine and saw the blinking light indicating that there were messages. She responded "yes, do you want me to play them?" I was more than eager to tell her yes because I had also turned the volume up on the answering machine before I left to make sure that she could hear Darren's voice loud and clear.

After I told her to play the messages, I walked towards the living room so I could watch her facial expression as she listened to the messages. She pressed the play button on the answering machine and heard "Hi T, it's me Darren. I was just calling you to say that I'm so sorry for getting mad at you for doing something with another man while we weren't together. I was a jerk and I hope that you can forgive me." She went to turn off the machine after the first message, but I yelled at her and told her to let it play. She couldn't even look me in the eyes after she heard the first one, but the next two messages forced her to walk out of the room and tell me "So, you found the tape. What now?" The only thing I could say to her was "Get out of my house!"

She asked me if I really wanted to do this. I told her that I've wanted to do this since this afternoon when I found out she had been meddling in my relationship with Darren. I had already packed all her belongings in an overnight bag that she left at my house. I picked up the bag and handed it to her and told her not to bother coming back to my house ever again. I told her that I would still be there for her when she adopted her children, but our relationship was over and I could never trust her again. She asked if we could talk about it and I told her a definite "no". I didn't want to hear her reasons for doing what she did. She was just too underhanded and cunning for me and I had enough.

After Tracey left my house that evening, I cried myself to sleep. I knew that I had just lost a friend in her, but I was mad at myself for allowing her to take advantage of my trust. My relationship with Darren was ruined because I was looking for immediate gratification for my sexual needs. I even pretended to be a lesbian for almost a year because of sex. I needed to reevaluate myself as a person. I knew that life wasn't all about sex and I wondered why it was always the primary thing in my life. I even started blaming myself for Phil's death. If I never slept with that lunatic, Vinny, Phil would have never gotten killed. I needed to talk to the only person I was comfortable enough with to give me guidance. I went to sleep that night hoping to talk to my brother, Will, first thing in the morning.

Chapter 48

Will and I had reconnected again after my skeletons were exposed on television. He was able to get passed some of the things that came to light during that turbulent period in my life. Will had moved to Florida and bought a nice home in Weston, a few miles from Fort Lauderdale. I had gone to his house a few times to visit and he had a cook-out for me once and he invited some of his friends. I noticed that Will was still quite the ladies man. Even though there were other football players at his house who were more recognizable for their talent on the field, the ladies were drawn more to Will than any of them for some reason.

I watched him in action and I noticed some of the moves that he was putting on the women. He was smooth and he couldn't help gloating about the fact that he was sleeping with many of those women. Watching him in action was fun and I couldn't understand how he had so many of his women in one place at one time. He told me that most of them knew about each other. Some of them were even getting angry when I gave Will a hug. Of course, he checked them after I checked them to make sure that they never disrespected his little sister.

But there was this one woman named Roxanne that my brother was seeing who was a Sex Therapist. To tell you the truth, I thought that bitch had too many problems of her own to be trying to help somebody else with their problems. She was always in competition with the other women who were around. All she talked about was the fact that she had attended an Ivy League university and that she had more to offer a man than most women. She swore that men were intimidated by her intelligence and only a few of them had enough balls to step to her because she was the whole package. I was thinking to myself, I'm glad I didn't pursue a doctorate in psychology because that chick was out of her mind and maybe being in school for too long make people lose their minds.

The whole time she was running her mouth, Will was laughing. As high and mighty as she wanted to act around the people at the party, Will told me he had that chick crawling on all fours acting like a dog around the house once. She was into freaky shit and she liked having him tie a dog collar around her neck and walk her around the house. That shit was almost unbelievable to me. He said she would raise her leg up like a dog and bark while he had sex with her doggy style.

When I spoke with my brother the morning after I gave Tracey the boot, he told me that I should talk to that crazy woman about my sexual problems. I knew he couldn't be serious. After all that he told me about her, he actually thought that I was gonna agree to see her? My brother pleaded with me and told that she was a well-known therapist in Miami and that her treatment methods had been featured in psychological journals all over the country. I was even more shocked to hear that this woman was a respectable therapist.

I finally agreed to go down to Miami to spend a week with my brother and give this crazy ass lady a try. This time when I got to the house, he didn't throw a party like he usually did. He wanted to spend time with me and talk about his life. My brother was getting tired of sleeping around with a bunch of women and he wanted to find the right one to settle down with. I almost laughed in his face when he told me that, but the serious look that he gave me convinced me that he was serious. My brother had a sexual addiction of his own and it was Roxanne, the psychotherapist, who helped him overcome his addiction. He told me her techniques were error proof and that I would start seeing results almost immediately.

That week, I spent most of my time with my brother and at Roxanne's office. I did see progress after the first couple of days, but every now and I then I busted out laughing in her office because of what my brother told me about her. Ms. Roxanne had some issues of her own that she needed to seek help for and I wondered if she was personally seeing a psychologist to help her work on herself. I heard that most therapists and psychologists are usually in need of psychological help themselves and Roxanne seemed like she could definitely use it.

Roxanne helped me focus on me as a person instead of my sexual needs. She pointed out that I was behaving like a monkey swinging through a jungle. She told me that her analysis was based on the fact that I told her that I had never been alone since I became an adult. When she broke down her analogy to me, it made a lot of sense. She explained to me that monkeys that swing in the jungle usually don't let go of a tree branch until they get their hands on another branch and I was doing the same thing with the people that I got involved with in my life.

We discussed that I was afraid of being by alone, so every time a person walked out of my life, I grabbed hold of a new one to replace them for security. She also noted that I was never a lesbian and I allowed the needy side of me to become emotionally involved in a relationship that meant nothing to me. She was right about the fact that I wasn't lesbian because even I knew it. She pointed out to me that I was not being fair to Tracey. I led Tracey to believe that we had a real relationship based on true feelings when all the while I was just trying to satisfy my own personal needs.

At first, I really didn't expect this woman to have any kind of in-depth input about anything, but true to her profession, she knew what she was doing. At the end of the week, I felt like a new person and Roxanne and I agreed to have our sessions over the phone until I returned to Florida. I developed profound respect for Roxanne and her profession as time went by and I'm now slowly but surely recovering from a sexual dependency that I created for myself. She told me that I wasn't just addicted to sex, but I was also dependent on sex because I wanted to be pleased all the time and sex was the tool that I used.

Chapter 49

I came back to New York feeling renewed. While I was on the plane, I tried to recall all the partners that I had slept with over the years and some of them were so insignificant, I couldn't even recall their names. My life had been a mess and I didn't even know it. The only person from my list that had any significance to me was my one and only Darren. I thought about what Roxanne said to me about using Tracey for my own needs and I made a promise to myself to apologize to her for leading her on. But first, I had to get in touch with Darren because he was the only person that I still wanted in my life, not just as a lover, but also as a friend.

Upon entering my house, I kicked my shoes off and laid my baggage down by the door in the kitchen from the garage entrance. I went upstairs to run my bubble bath. I tried to create an atmosphere that was relaxed and soothing. I had picked up a copy of this book called Meeting Ms. Right by this young author from the bookstore at the airport, but I didn't get a chance to open it because I was too busy thinking about what I was going to do with my life on the plane. I took my clothes off and dropped them to the floor in the bedroom. I went and grabbed the copy of Meeting Ms. Right out of my purse, so I could read it while I relaxed in the tub.

I was in the tub for almost two hours because I couldn't put the book down. The only reason I even stopped reading was because the water in the tub had gotten cold and I started to shiver and had goose bumps all over my body. I found myself laughing out loud at the silly stunts that Malcolm and Dexter were pulling in that book. Dexter even reminded me a little bit of my brother. He was the player of all players while his best friend, Malcolm chose to remain a virgin until he met the right woman. I'm not even gonna front, the sexual scenes in that book had me playing with myself in the tub and it was all good because my therapist told me that masturbation was perfectly normal and natural.

After I ran the water out of the tub, I rinsed off in the shower. I stepped out of the shower feeling clean and I couldn't wait to finish the book. I dried off with a towel, I threw on my pajamas then I called the local Chinese restaurant to deliver some shrimp fried rice and chicken and broccoli to my house. I put away my baggage while I wait for my food to arrive.

After I ate, I poured myself a glass of wine and I curled in front of my fire place to finish my book. I was happy to find that the book was not disappointing at the end. The author kept my attention from beginning to end and I've been talking about that book and recommending it to anyone who would listen every time the subject of reading came up. I had been trying to make time to go to the bookstore to pick up another book called Neglected Souls by the same author that I heard great things about. I guess my time will be occupied from reading all these great books that this guy is writing. I'm hearing that there's going to be a sequel to Neglected Souls called Neglected No More coming soon from him as well.

I realized that I even forgot to pick up the phone to call Tracey to apologize I was so caught up in that book. I had made a promise and I wanted to keep it. The following night while I was home, I picked up the phone to dial Tracey's number. After a short ring, an automated voice came on to say "the number you are trying to call is no longer in service, please check the number and dial again" and I did that. I checked the number and I dialed again and it was the same response. Tracey had changed her number, but I decided to buy her a card and put it in the mail. I knew that she could change her number, but she couldn't change her address. She owned the home where she lived and there was no way she was gonna give that home up because of a bad relationship with me.

That house was her pride and joy. I mailed the card to Tracey never expecting to hear from her again. I simply told her that I was sorry about the way things turned out and that I didn't mean to lead her on.

Chapter 50

While I was trying my best to learn that spending time alone was essential to overcoming my sexual dependency, I also grew closer to my mother and father in the process. Since Will lived out of state, they became my best friends. I went away on gambling trips to Atlantic City with them, we sometimes went out to dinner, we went out to see a few plays on Broadway and my daddy was happy to see that his little girl was not such a bad person after all.

My parents wanted to know if I was content with myself and if I had heard from Darren. I told them that I was happy, but I hadn't heard from him. My mother could tell that I missed Darren and wanted to see him. After I explained to her the whole incident about Tracey's evil doings regarding Darren, she urged me to call him to make amends, but not before she forced me to tell her about my lesbian experiences. My mother couldn't believe that I had been with a woman.

While it would have been a lot more shocking to my dad, my mother was only a little surprised. She had come to expect these things from me and nothing I told her was gonna shock her heart anymore. I also told my mother that I used to hear when she and my dad were going at it when I was a little girl. She jokingly told me that whenever she was yelling God's name, it was because they were praying. I asked her if they still pray the same way, she said "God never takes religion away. He might slow down the ability to pray as people get older, but I still scream his name at least three times a week. My mother was giving a little too much information than I cared to know.

I knew that my mom would keep my little lesbian affair from my dad and my brother. I could always trust her to have my back. My father was not ready to hear about any girl on girl action coming from his daughter. He didn't have any problems with homosexuals as long as neither of his children was gay. My daddy was coming of age, but he didn't come far enough. He couldn't even understand how a woman could be with more than one man in her lifetime unless her husband was dead. My daddy married my mother when she was still a virgin and he expected me to stay a virgin until I married. However, his expectation for my brother was different. According to him, Will needed to go out and gain experience for his future wife. There were just some things about my dad that I accepted would never change. I love him regardless.

Chapter 51

I was about to make a decision that I was struggling with. I wanted to heed my mother's advice about calling Darren, but I also thought about the last time I tried to surprise him and I ended up with a little surprise of my own. I knew that Darren wasn't going to magically appear on my front door, but I didn't really have the courage to call him. All kinds of stupid things went through my mind as I sat on the couch with my cordless phone in hand dialing the first three digits then hanging up. I would pick up the phone again and dial five of the numbers and I'd lose my courage and I would hang it up again. Finally, I said to myself, "There could only be two outcomes from the phone call, he'd either speak to me or he'd hang up the phone on me." I was ready to let the balls fall where they may.

It seemed like it took forever for the phone to finally ring after I dialed the ten-digit number to Darren's phone. The phone rang once, then it rang twice and just before I decided to hang up again, Darren picked up. He recognized my number right away on his caller-id. He eased my apprehensions when he said "how ya doing, stranger?" Darren actually sounded happy to hear from me. I told him that I was doing well and that I was calling him because I wanted to talk to him. Before I could start my next sentence Darren told me that he's been missing me and he was hoping to receive a phone call from me since he saw me at the car wash. I was happy to hear that, but I told him that I didn't want to call him until after I did some work on myself. "What's wrong with you?" he asked. That's why I was crazy about Darren; He still saw nothing wrong with me as a person even after what I had put him through.

Darren and I continued to talk and I told him that I went to see a therapist about my sexual dependency and that I wanted to work on everything else that I thought was wrong with me. Out of the blue, he asked me if I was single and I couldn't wait to tell him that I was annoyingly single. I told him that my last relationship didn't work out because my heart wasn't in it. I told him that Tracey and I were on different wavelengths and I had to discover myself and I found out that wasn't what I wanted. He asked if Tracey was somebody new that I started dating after him and I told him "yes". He said "I guess Tracey stole my girl from me. He must've been a great guy for him to steal you away from me for so long." I told him Tracey was not a he, but a she. Darren was silent on the phone for a few minutes, but he came back and said "so, I forced you to turn lesbian?" I told him he had nothing to do with me running into the arms of a woman. It was my old self not wanting to be alone.

Darren and I talked for a long time that night and I told him about all my sexual partners and how I had been dependent on sex since we were in high school and that I sought help for it at my brother's urging. Darren was happy to hear that I was trying to change my way of life and he told me that he would always be there to support me. Before I got off the phone with Darren, I wanted to find out if he was single. When I asked him if there was anyone special in his life, he hesitated at first, but he came back and said "I only have room in my life for one special woman and that woman will always be you. I was just waiting for your call." My face lit up like a big Christmas tree standing in front of the White House in the middle of December after he said that.

I was happy that Darren was willing to give our relationship another chance, but this time I told him that I wanted to take things slowly. Darren and I started hanging out again and this time we spent most of our time getting to know each other. We weren't prudes, but we never went all the way with our sexual urges. There was so much to do in New York that we hadn't done, we took our time to familiarize ourselves with the city and did things that most people from other countries who visited the city did. We went to the Empire state building for the first time, we visited the Statue of Liberty, we went to the New York Metropolitan museum, we went to the Brooklyn museum to check out an exhibit by Jean Michel Basquiat and we discovered Prospect Park in Brooklyn.

Darren and I spent a lot of time doing outdoorsy things to keep from acting out our sexual urges. We went to Central Park for a picnic one day and we ended up watching a free concert by this popular singing group. There was no limit to the things we did as Darren and I became reacquainted. Even something as simple as a train ride from Long Island to Manhattan from Manhattan to Brooklyn and from Brooklyn to the Bronx was fun to us. We never rode the train to Queens because it was easy to drive from our house to Queens.

One day we went to the Green Acres mall in Queens and we acted like two teenagers the whole day. We kept messing around with the undercover security guards at Macy's. We acted like we were trying to steal clothes from Macy's and they kept following us around while trying to act like they were regular customers. We knew it was because we were black. When we were leaving the store Darren and I flipped them the bird.

We even drove to Coney Island to take a ride on that old cyclone and the Merry Go Round that looked like it was about to fall apart. The hotdogs at Coney Island were the best hot dogs that we had ever eaten. Spending time with Darren was a lot of fun and we appreciated every moment that we spent together.

Chapter 52

I asked Darren if he wanted to go out on a special date with me a couple of months after we had been hanging out. It was the upcoming Friday and he told that he'd be honored. I was so happy that evening, I ended up staying on the phone with Darren for four hours; we talked about how we were going to make things work better this time around and there wasn't going to be any more secrets between us and everything would be up for discussion and consideration. Darren had made my night and I went to bed hugging my pillow like it was his body that I enveloped myself in.

I was looking forward so much to my date with Darren I didn't know what to do with myself. I felt like a teenager all over again going out with the big man on campus. Darren had made my dream come true when he picked up the phone and spoke to me in his sexy signature tone the night that I called him. My panties were all wet while we spoke that night. It had nothing to do with any sexual dependency. I wanted to hear Darren's voice and listen to his sweet words that were always so soothing to me. I wanted my man back and I was going to do everything and anything to make things work this time around.

I had called Darren at work earlier in the day to ask him what I should wear on our date and he told me to wear something that was definitely sexy. I could just picture his eyes when he said that. I knew exactly what I was going to wear. I had seen this nice dress at Ann Taylor that I thought would just have Darren falling all over me. It was black with a wrap around strap that tied to the side and because I had a lot of curves, the contours of my shape would be highlighted through the dress. I also bought these black open toed sexy stilettos from this exclusive boutique in Manhattan. I made a trip to the nail salon to get a manicure and pedicure because Darren always complimented my pedicured toes back when we were dating.

Our date was set for eight o'clock and I was ready by seven fifty. Darren was always prompt and I did not want to keep him waiting that night. I wanted to turn a new leaf in every aspect of my life and being on time was one of them. My door bell rang at exactly eight o'clock. When I opened the door, Darren gave me a big hug and he handed me a bouquet of tulips. He smelled good, he looked good and I was wet. I went up to my room to grab my matching purse and coat before we left.

That night, Darren was a total gentleman. He held the door open for me in the car and at the restaurant. He ordered my food after I told him what I wanted and he checked to make sure that I was okay every fifteen minutes. Darren was always a gentleman, but he had become quite the romantic since I last saw him. Over dinner, we talked about our lives and how many kids that we saw in our future. We even discussed the names for our children. Darren was adamant about calling his son junior and I told him that I wanted to name my son after my father. At the end, we agreed to disagree and I told Darren that we'd figure all that out when the children actually arrive.

Sometime during dinner, the conversation shifted from family to fantasy. I wanted to know Darren's fantasies because I wanted to help fulfill them. I thought he was going to be creative with his answer, but just like a typical man, his fantasy was to be with not two, but three women at once. His logic behind it was to have one woman riding him, one sitting on his face that he'd be eating and the third one would be the spare for when one of the other two women needed a break. This fool really thought he had enough energy to satisfy three women at once. Darren thought he was an expert with the tongue and even gave more credit to his tongue than his dick. I loved his tongue and all, but I would take his twelve inches any day over his tongue.

We were so comfortable talking about his fantasy, I was a little at ease when it was my turn to tell him about mine. When I told Darren that I wanted to be with two men at once, his demeanor changed completely. He gave me this look like I wasn't supposed to be thinking about being with two men. I proceeded very carefully to tell him that it was just a fantasy and that I would never expect it to ever happen. I made sure he understood that he would never live out his fantasy to be with three women as long as he was with me. For some reason, I didn't think Darren accepted my explanation. The look on his face was enough to cut right through me when I mentioned being with two men. Darren has a little bad streak in him as well and sometimes it comes out when I least expect it.

I didn't really want to get into an argument with Darren, so I changed the subject to something light. We started cracking on the couple sitting across from us. They were a wrinkly looking old man wearing a toupee and a young woman who looked like a younger version of Anna Nicole Smith. The man looked like he was going to have a heart attack at any moment. Darren was cracking on him saying that she probably had to change his diaper three or four times on the way to the restaurant.

That woman was all over him trying to be overly affectionate in public like she was putting on a show for a private-eye watching them from afar. The old man had a hard time hearing everything that his waiter was saying to him and he spoke his thoughts out loud like he was deaf. At one point, he called the waiter an idiot who didn't listen. If I were him, I wouldn't have bothered to eat the food. He would've been lucky if he only found boogers in his food. He was so rude; I wouldn't have put it past the waiter to have his food cooked with urine.

Darren and I had had enough of the old man and it was time for us to leave the restaurant. He paid the bill and left a generous tip for the waiter before we left. I wrapped myself into Darren's arms as we waited for the valet to retrieve his car. He gave me a couple of little pecks to show me that he still cared about me. However, he wouldn't let go of my comment about the two men. He brought it up again and I had to keep telling him that it was just a fantasy.

Chapter 53

On the way to the house in the car, I kept rubbing Darren's thighs trying to get him aroused and he told me that if I continued, he was going to give me something that I couldn't handle when I got home. "Since your fantasy is to be with two men when we get to your house, I'm gonna introduce you to my alter ego, Da'Ron. I'm gonna tear your ass up until you can't take no more", he said. I smiled at him because I knew he meant it. There was determination in his voice and I knew Darren had never let me down before.

When we arrived at my house, I invited Darren inside. He sat in the living room while I went to the kitchen to get us a bottle of wine and two glasses. We were watching an old rerun of Sanford and Son on television and laughing at Fred calling Lamont "a big dummy". By the time the show ended, Darren and I were on the couch all over each other. He was in his undershirt while my dress was coming up above my head and totally off my body seconds later. I hadn't been with anybody in a few months and I couldn't wait for Darren to put his hands on me. He was rubbing my tities and kissing me like he had never kissed me before. Darren was passionate, efficient and moist with his tongue. He went from rubbing my breasts to caressing my ass then to sucking my breasts all over the couch.

I unzipped his pants and I pulled out my favorite part of his body that I missed so much and I wrapped my lips around all twelve inches of it. I sucked and caressed it like I hadn't seen it in months. In fact, I hadn't. I placed his dick between my tits and held them together tight for him to fuck my tities. He humped my tities back and forth as I tried to get my lips around the head of his dick between strokes. I was so hot for him, I told him to hold my breasts together so I could use my fingers to rub my clit. Darren sat on my chest with his dick extended into my mouth and his finger inside my pussy while I wind all over his finger until I came. He wasn't done with me yet. He lifted me up from the couch and sat me down on the top part of the couch where people rest their backs when they sit. He spread my legs open and knelt on the couch to eat me until I started screaming so loud that I thought my neighbors were going to call the cops.

With his dick extended to the maximum twelve inches that he was blessed with, Darren picked me up and held me up by my thighs with my legs spread open and my back against his stomach, he started fucking me like I was a gymnast in flight from a somersault. He carried me upstairs to the bedroom while in the same position. He stood in front of the mirror in the bedroom with my legs spread wide open to watch his dick go in and out of me. He held me up like a curling bar from a weight room and each time he brought me down, I could feel his whole dick penetrating me with strength and desire. With his body perspiring about a bucket of sweats a second, Darren placed me down on the edge of the bed on my back with my legs wide open in a split position and he continued to fuck me with this rage in his eyes because he wanted to feel the wrath of his total manhood dominating my pussy.

I came so many times I didn't know how much longer I could take Darren inside of me. He pulled me near him, with my leg leaning up on his arm for support. He unleashed himself inside of me gaining maximum penetration. Darren stroked and stroked and stroked me harder until I felt his combustion all over my stomach. But he wasn't done yet. Since I asked to be with two men, Darren wanted to show me the equivalent of two men in him. I know that I would never make that mistake again with Darren. He fucked me like he had something to prove. And I will never give a man with a twelve-inch dick and knows how to use it, a reason to prove anything to me ever again.

Chapter 54

I know that most people won't believe that my story is at all possible in the real world, but sometimes that's the hardest thing that we have to deal with. Everything seems so far fetched, most of the time we believe that they're impossible. With the support of my family and Darren, I'm coping everyday with my new life. But the events that took place in my life had to happen in order for me to change as a person.

I want people to know that it isn't always those folks who come from dysfunctional families that develop certain dependencies and addictions. My mother and father were model parents, but somehow my brother and I managed to developed sexual habits that were incomprehensible to most people. Open communication with my brother also helped make me realize that I was not alone in my struggles. Thank goodness I have the kind of people in my life who cared enough about me to help me gain control of my life again, but not everyone is so lucky.

I also had to realize the elements of narcissism that was steering my life in the wrong direction. The constant search for confirmation of who I was and the immediate search for self-gratification were things that I had to learn to let go and deal with. I was like a baby who cried constantly and someone had to immediately put a bottle or a pacifier in my mouth to soothe me. It's the closest metaphor that I can come up with for my sexual dependency and need for control.

Some people don't realize how devastating that sex can be and how it can sometimes make us lose control of our lives. While sexual gratification can be the ultimate high, however, at the same time we need to be careful not to allow it to control who we are as human beings. We can't deny that sex can be great with the right person, but you shouldn't allow it to control your life or use it to control anyone else's life.

Well, that was my story. Just remember to do everything in moderation as I'm learning everyday. Darren will still be tearing my ass up and I wouldn't have it any other way, but this time around I will try to be modest and enjoy it day by day.

Have a good day and great sex!